BACK
on the
MAP

Also by Lisa Ann Scott:
School of Charm

BACK
on the
MAP

Lisa Ann Scott

Sky Pony Press
New York

Sky Pony Press books may be purchased in bulk at special discounts for sales promotion, corporate gifts, fund-raising, or educational purposes. Special editions can also be created to specifications. For details, contact the Special Sales Department, Sky Pony Press, 307 West 36th Street, 11th Floor, New York, NY 10018 or info@skyhorsepublishing.com.

Sky Pony® is a registered trademark of Skyhorse Publishing, Inc.®, a Delaware corporation.

Visit our website at www.skyponypress.com.

10 9 8 7 6 5 4 3 2 1

Library of Congress Cataloging-in-Publication Data is available on file.

Cover illustration by Christiane Engel

Print ISBN: 978-1-5107-1353-6
E-book ISBN: 978-1-5107-1354-3

Printed in the United States of America

Interior design by Joshua L. Barnaby

BACK on the MAP

To my wonderful editor, Rachel Stark, for taking in my orphaned book and loving it like her own. And especially for demanding the very best from it.

CHAPTER 1

It was a day for high fives and cheers, but I sat in class with that nervous hum buzzing inside me like a warning bell. Like a hive of bees. Sometimes big things happened on the last day of school. Bad things. Like getting bounced to a new town because we'd become too much again. Any minute now, we could get called down to the principal's office and find Grauntie waiting with our stuff. I could just imagine the horrible message booming through all the speakers in school: *Penny and Parker Porter, it's time for you to leave.*

I closed my eyes and pictured all my things neatly folded on the bed. I'd left them there so Grauntie wouldn't miss anything if she decided to pack up for us. I lost my only photo of Mama three years ago, when Cousin Janice showed up with our stuff in garbage bags on the last day of school. Uncle Dean had come to take us that time. I'm not even sure who it would be this time.

We'd used up all our relatives. The ones we knew about, anyway. We didn't know our daddy's name, or where he was. No one did.

Ever since that day three years ago, the last day of school's been a great big worry day. Even more so this year, the way Grauntie was getting. So today I had everything ready to go, except for my pink hair clip shaped like a rabbit. I'd searched all over, and I couldn't find it, so I'd have to let it go. But my two most important things were right with me, stashed in my desk. I touched the book and the letter and felt better, knowing they were there. At least I wouldn't lose those if we got bounced.

Tick. Tock. Tick. Tock. The darn clock by the door was beating away the moments like a drum. Half an hour of fifth grade left. Seemed like time was slowing down while my heart was speeding up. And all I could do was wait, wait, wait.

I wondered if Parker was sitting in his class feeling the same way. Probably not. I did the worrying for the both of us. I sighed. Waiting for a bad thing is much harder than waiting for a good thing.

I fanned myself and looked around the stuffy room. Sally Kenney was snoozing, ready to topple over. No one was squirming and chattering or bouncing in their seats.

You'd think they'd be ready to bust out the door smack dab into summer break, but not the kids in this town.

Even so, I didn't want to leave New Hope. Parker and I had never lasted this long anywhere else, and things were nice and easy here. No one took much notice of us. No people picking on Parker and his weird ways. No kids refusing to play with us because we looked different. Every other town we'd lived in had been full of busybodies, always nosing around. "These white folks are your family?" "What are you? Mexican? Black? Mixed?" Most of those folks didn't like not getting answers. Well, guess what? I didn't like having none to give.

Not that life in New Hope was perfect. Grauntie was old, and her memory was breaking off in bits. And the whole town was still moping around about the Great Disappointment: New Hope's Finest, the great big building that was supposed to reopen as something brand new but never did. It still sat empty, high atop a hill in the middle of town, its face to the row of shops on Main Street and its back up against the highway.

Even here in the classroom you could see it. I shifted in my seat, staring out the window at it while I waited for school to wind down. It had once been an orphanage. It was on a big plot of land surrounded by a tall wooden fence, but you could still see the top half of the building. The sign on the roof read NEW HOPE'S FINEST, with an empty space after "FINEST," still waiting for that final word to be painted in. Ten years later, that space on the sign, like the building itself, sat there empty and forgotten. Unwanted.

No wonder people here were sad all the time, with that great big misfortune staring down at everyone.

Mr. Hanes didn't notice me not paying attention. Maybe 'cause it was his final day, ever, at our school. He was more excited than the students.

"One more thing before you leave," he said. He pulled out a file from the bottom drawer. "I want to give you back the just-for-fun sheets you filled out on the first day of school."

Kids shifted in their seats. Most of them yawned.

"That's neat," I said, just so he'd know at least one person was listening.

"It sure is, Penny." The color in Mr. Hanes's cheeks was blooming with the promise of leaving New Hope.

Parker once told me no one else saw folks in shades like I did. But I had to believe someone else out there could spot a person filled up with color, or find folks practically drained dry. Most everyone in New Hope was nothing but walking, talking, black-and-white sketches. Sometimes they seemed to move in slow motion, too. Suppose that's what happens when a town's been stewing in sadness for so long.

To me, it didn't matter if a person was mixed, or what their skin looked like. What mattered was how strong your color glowed. Those poor folks in New Hope didn't glow at all. But I did, and so did Parker. We were solid color, through and through.

Mama had always been full color, until she got sick. Then she faded and faded until she was gone. I could still remember her face: her green, green eyes, her crooked front tooth. She had bushy, copper-colored hair, just like mine. The same shade as a penny. The reason for my name.

Our skin was different, though. So many times I set my arm next to hers, comparing her snowy skin with my light-brown skin. Parker had the same color skin as me. I figured that meant Daddy must've had darker skin, to mix with Mama's and make ours. Suppose he had freckles, too, cause Mama didn't—and I do. Lots of them. I tried counting once, but had to stop at five hundred fifty-two. Somehow, lucky Parker was freckle-free.

I examined my arms, imagining the shapes the dots

made, while Mr. Hanes passed out our sheets. "Here you go, Penny."

"Thanks, sir." I took my stack of sheets from him. They were filled with questions about my family, and my dreams for the future.

I ripped them into tiny strips. Not 'cause I was mad about the questions. I hadn't answered most of them, anyway. I was just itching to make confetti. How exciting to have a celebration too big for words and applause, like Mr. Hanes's last day of school in New Hope—you needed a flurry of paper in the sky to show how important it was. Plus, it settled my nerves some, as I worried about it being *my* last day in New Hope, too.

I kept shredding my sheets and dropping the tiny bits in my empty lunch bag. Once I finished the dreams and family sheets, I tore up the family tree. It was blank. Didn't have enough family to fill it in with.

But I'd been working on one at home—a secret one. The one I wished was real. *I come from proud, great people. The people on my tree.*

I blew into the bag like it was a paper balloon and shook the confetti inside, waiting for the bell to ring in three, two, one . . . "Happy very last day of school, Mr.

Hanes!" I popped it just as the bell rang. A tiny cloud of confetti rained down, sprinkling my desk and the floor.

"Why, thank you, Penny," said Mr. Hanes.

I smiled at him, keeping my lips pressed together. I wasn't one to flash my teeth, especially seeing as how most of 'em were crooked.

The kids shuffled out of the room, some of the confetti sticking to their shoes.

I waved goodbye to my friends Carly and Chase. They lived on our street, and sometimes, if their color glowed enough, Parker and I could drag them along on our adventures. They waved back, but left the room without a word.

Then I waited. And waited and waited for the principal's voice to boom through the speaker next to the clock. I held my breath and crossed my fingers. *Please let us stay here.*

CHAPTER 2

The speaker was quiet. The classroom phone didn't jingle, either. Relief whooshed through me; we were in the clear. For now.

I stayed put so I could talk business with Mr. Hanes. He was full color now, but it was faint, like he'd been filled in by a kid pressing lightly with his crayons to make them last longer.

"What are you going to do with all this stuff?" I asked, once the room was empty.

"Most of it will stay for the new teacher. But the rest," he said with a shrug, "I'll just pack up and leave for the janitor to take care of."

"I could save him the work and take what you don't want for our trading cart. I brought it to school today. It's locked up on the bike rack."

He smiled and shook a finger at me. "That's a great

idea. I'll call Mrs. Johnson, and she can tell Parker to bring it in." He picked up the phone.

"Sounds good." Schools usually kept me and Parker in separate classes, 'cause we distracted each other.

Mr. Hanes hung up the phone and pointed to the pots by the windows. "Why don't you take the plants, too?"

"Lots of folks will like those." I surveyed the room and stared at the poster of a cat clinging to a tree limb that said, HANG IN THERE, BABY!

"You can have all those posters, too. The new teacher will want to put up their own things." He pulled the tacks out and laid the posters flat on a desk.

"You should probably get rid of these tacks so no one steps on them. Want me to help out with that?" Thumbtacks would make perfect eyes on my tin can critters. I always found a use for things cast aside. It was my talent.

"Sure. And take any of those books you'd like," Mr. Hanes said, pointing to the bookcase in the corner.

I'd take 'em all; they'd be good for trading. The ones I didn't keep, that is. Books were as good as friends.

I heard the squeaky wheels of the trading cart coming down the hall. Parker walked into the room and gave me the handle of the first wagon. There was a second wagon, just like it, tied to the back.

When I thanked him, Parker shoved his hands in his pockets and nodded. Parker was either silent or a chatterbox, no in-between. When we stayed with Mama's grandma, Nanny Gladys, a few years back, she always called him an odd bird.

Mr. Hanes set a box of paint bottles and craft supplies in my wagon. Parker collected the plants.

I walked over to the huge map of North Carolina on the back wall, its corners tattered and curling. "What's going to happen to this?"

"It's yours. No need for it now. I'm leaving North Carolina today. U-Haul's packed and hitched to my car outside. One year in this town was more than enough." Mr. Hanes was probably going to get a speeding ticket on the way out of town, he was so eager to skedaddle.

I nodded. Since we'd be saving the janitor work, it was a fair trade to take the map. I stared up at it, looking for New Hope. I knew it was between Winston-Salem and Asheville, but I couldn't find it. "Where are we?"

"New Hope's not on the map," Mr. Hanes said.

"Why not? Shouldn't every place be on the map?" How had I not noticed that before?

"There's not room for every little town and village." He shrugged. "New Hope's not big enough. Not important enough. No reason for anybody to be looking for it."

That felt like a kick to the gut. Without a place on the map, couldn't a town get swept away? Forgotten? I scanned the map for the other places Parker and I had lived: Old Fort with Mama's mama, Granny Lynn; Black Creek with our Nanny Gladys, the crabby old lady; Delway with Mama's cousin Gert and her seven kids; Keener, with Mama's other cousin Janice; and then Woodland with Mama's brother, who didn't keep us but four months. None of those places were on the map, either.

Parker stood with his arms wrapped around a big, leafy plant, staring at the map, too.

Then a thought started beating my brain, thumping and pulsing faster and louder. It was so huge I had to sit down from the pressure of it. Parker and I had never lived anywhere big enough or important enough to be put on the map. No one had ever pushed a thumbtack into the thick paper to mark the place we'd called home.

I blew out a breath so the idea wouldn't swallow me whole. If you couldn't put a pin in a place like New Hope, how could I ever expect us to be tacked to one place? Parker and I needed to live somewhere that was on the map to keep us from being pulled to the next forgotten town. A town special enough to hold us.

I stood. "We've got to get New Hope on the map!" I cried. It was the key to staying. The truth of it hummed in my brain, so loud it hurt. My best ideas always hurt. That's how I knew when a thing was important. And getting New Hope on the map was more important than anything. I could feel the truth of it rattling in my bones: *Get on the map, and you'll never be bounced again.*

I'd have to put Sacagawea on my secret family tree right away. Since she'd gone with Lewis and Clark on their journey to map out the unknown western territory, her skills would be good to have. She helped them make their way across the land. And she was only seventeen! Without her, maybe Lewis and Clark couldn't have charted and claimed the west for America.

I'd read her story dozens of times in my *Notable People* book, which was sitting safely in my desk so I wouldn't lose it. It was my number-two most important thing, since Mama used to read it to me and Parker. I knew all the people's stories by heart. Sacagawea would be a fine,

fine person to have on my family tree, and a big help with anything related to maps, for sure.

Now, I wasn't absolutely certain she was kin, but since I knew nothing about my daddy there was no way of knowing she *didn't* belong on my tree. I looked down at my light-brown hands. That color could be from Sacagawea. I could be from the Shoshone tribe. So, she would join the amazing people I'd been adding during the past two years, ever since the first time one of my teachers passed out a family tree sheet and I realized mine was half empty, sadder than a Charlie Brown Christmas tree. I closed my eyes and thought I could feel her in my heart. *I am the descendant of a great explorer.*

I didn't have a real family that loved me, but I had a wonderful imaginary one that did.

Feeling inspired by my link to Sacagawea, I stared at that map on Mr. Hanes's wall for a while, tracing my fingers over the smooth paper, wondering exactly where New Hope would be.

Mr. Hanes walked over, shaking his head. "Get New Hope on the map." He chuckled. "Good luck with that. This town can't even get a proper road sign on the highway. I always figured once you lose hope, it's gone forever."

He was probably right about that. Years ago, before Parker and I had moved to New Hope, someone had used spray paint to cross out New Hope on the highway sign and write No Hope underneath it. That was the first thing we'd seen as we were driven into town, the bright-yellow paint glowing in the blur of all those green trees as we whizzed by.

"I can't believe someone did that to the sign," I said, mostly to myself.

"I imagine people were upset when . . . you know." Mr. Hanes's color was fading a bit from even mentioning The Great Disappointment.

"People need to get over that. It's been, what, ten years?" Mama had died six years ago, and I'd moved on. And that was way worse than The Great Disappointment.

"Well, this is an unusual little town, I'll tell you that." He brought over a box of odds and ends and set it in my wagon. "I'm just going to consider myself lucky I've spent my year here without finding a doom painting on my doorstep."

I blinked at him. "Doom painting?" I whispered the words to myself and got chill bumps. "What's that?"

His color drained some more. "Folks don't mention doom paintings much, but one of the other teachers told me about them. Joe Jinx paints them and leaves them on people's doorsteps overnight. Something bad always happens after a painting shows up. That's why they're called doom paintings. And that's why he's called Joe Jinx." He looked around the room like he was nervous. "And that's one of the reasons I'm leaving this town."

My mouth hung open. "I can't believe I've never heard about them."

His eyebrows rose. "I'm not surprised at all. Some people think just talking about them will bring you one."

I clamped my mouth shut, and my mind spun, thinking about the very idea of cursed paintings. What kind of person would paint them? Someone crazy? Someone mean? "I've never heard of Joe Jinx, either," I said. And here I thought I'd met everyone in New Hope.

"Sure, he's around. Lives in that big white house on the edge of town."

I nodded, understanding now why he was a stranger. No one ever answered the door when we stopped by that house with the trading cart. So we quit going. There were lots of old, abandoned homes around town, and we skipped them all.

Mr. Hanes continued, in a voice like he was telling a ghost story, "Joe left his first doom painting on the front door of New Hope's Finest, and the very next day the developers disappeared, along with the money to finish the project. He's been painting them ever since. And that's why I'm leaving right now, and never coming back. With my luck, I'd find one on my doorstep tomorrow morning, and my life would be ruined." His color was returning as he gathered his things and headed for the door. "Goodbye, kids."

I waved at him. "So long, Mr. Hanes. Maybe someday you can come back. If we get New Hope on the map. I mean, *when* we do. 'Cause we will."

He laughed. "I hope you do, kids. Lock the door when you're done in here."

I nodded. "Yes, sir. I'll just get this map, and then we'll leave."

Parker and I got the map down, and I noticed the name and address of the map company printed in tiny letters at the top: CHARTER MAPS IN RALEIGH. I rolled it up. Parker looked at me and raised his eyebrows.

I knew what he was wondering. I blew out a long breath, like it could take all my anxious feelings with it. "I don't know how we'll get New Hope back on the map. But we will." Because if we didn't, we'd get bounced right into the system, just like Nanny Gladys had warned us so many times.

But I'd never let us go into the system. We'd run away together before the two of us got split up. I'd never let us be forced to live with folks who didn't want us.

CHAPTER 3

We packed everything into the trading cart, and I grabbed my book and my letter from the desk. I put the letter in my pocket and tucked the book into my bookbag. I'd been so excited, loading up the trading cart, I'd forgotten for a while to worry about finding our stuff packed up at home. Maybe Grauntie was waiting until we got there to give us the bad news.

Parker put on his sunglasses as we stepped outside. He didn't like bright lights. To be honest, the sun didn't shine very often in New Hope. It was usually tucked behind the clouds, like it was snoozing every time our bit of the earth passed by. Like we weren't important enough to peer at. But Parker didn't want to take a chance that it might peek out, so he always wore his sunglasses outdoors.

He slid on his winter gloves—he hated the smell the metal handle left on his skin—and then grabbed on to the cart. "Your hair clip is behind your dresser."

"Thanks." I didn't even ask how he knew I was looking for it—or where it was, for that matter. Parker could find stuff you didn't even know you were missing. It was like magic.

We pulled the wagon train home, taking turns 'cause it was heavy. A tight, tight knot was building in my chest as I wondered if we'd find our bags waiting in the living room. People seemed to feel better about shipping us off once school let out, since it didn't "disrupt our learning." Like they should get a medal for sticking with us till summer.

"Think we're getting bounced?" Parker asked. "Maybe we could ask to go back with Uncle Dean. He always had ice cream in the freezer." He sounded like he wasn't even worried. He had no idea how hard it was, being in charge of us both.

I stopped and shook a finger at him. "Parker Porter, you know what Mama told us. We don't ask for handouts or help, and we certainly aren't going to ask to be part of a family. A real family just wants you, no begging required."

Parker kicked a rock down the road until it bounced out of sight. "Wonder where we'll go next, then."

"Hush," I said. I didn't want to tell him the truth: that we were out of options. That if Grauntie didn't want us anymore, we'd be living in the wild lickety-split. "We want to stay here. Once we get New Hope back on the map, we won't have to worry about moving around no more."

Parker stuck out his bottom lip. "I guess. I just liked it best at Uncle Dean's. That's all."

"And he shipped us off," I reminded him in a nasty tone.

He crossed his arms and looked away from me. "Wouldn't hurt to ask if we could come back." His voice had a nasty tinge to it.

"Yes, it would." I sighed. Thank goodness Mama had put me in charge. She said so in the letter she wrote me from the hospital, before she died. That was the number-one most important thing I owned. I could never, ever lose that.

It wasn't a long letter, but it was stuffed with serious things. Besides telling me I was in charge of Parker since I'd been born a few minutes before him, Mama had written that she was sorry for leaving us, and warned me that life isn't fair—boy, was she right about that one. Plus, the letter had her three rules for getting by:

#1: Don't expect too much from the world. That way, you'll never be disappointed.

#2: Don't ask for help. We're not a charity case.

#3: You should never, ever have to ask someone to love you.

I always, always wished there was a page two of that letter, where she told me something about my daddy. At least one tiny little bit of information. Where was he? What great things did he do? I didn't even know his name. No one did—trust me, I'd asked everyone. All the relatives on Mama's mama's side. "I don't know who your daddy is," cousin Janice had told us at a family party. "Darlene would never tell anyone. Broke her mama's heart coming home pregnant with you two. Such a disappointment." The other relatives frowned at us and shook their heads when she said that. I never knew who was the disappointment though—Mama or me and Parker.

We walked on silently, past the cattails growing in ditches along the road. Parker wouldn't look at me, probably still mad I wouldn't ask Uncle Dean to take us back. We didn't argue often. Left a bad feeling in my tummy when we did. Usually, he agreed with whatever I told him.

Parker would never be okay on his own. He needed my help settling in to each new place so we didn't cause much of a fuss. After Mama died, the first place we stayed was with Mama's mama, Granny Lynn. We didn't know her much, but I got excited, thinking we'd be there for good. Turns out we gave her too many migraines—and too many reminders of what Granny Lynn always said was her daughter's biggest shame, having two brown children out of wedlock.

I thought that was strange. Seemed like we'd be a nice reminder of Mama. Her only reminder. But, no, she shipped us to *her* mama, Nanny Gladys. She kept us till the end of the school year and complained the whole time we were there. I didn't even bother getting hopeful the next few times we got bounced. We just didn't fit right in Mama's family. Maybe 'cause they were all snowy white and we weren't?

At least Grauntie didn't seem to mind us. Maybe 'cause we did most of the work. Heck, maybe she'd just forgotten how to be mean. As we came in sight of her house, I noticed the grass was knee-high in the front yard. We'd need someone to cut it soon—if we were still here. I could trade for that. But most yards 'round the house were overgrown. It was like the town of New Hope, North Carolina, had fallen asleep one day and never woken up. The two of us just weren't a problem here, with the boarded-up houses and crumbling roads. It was the perfect place for two kids no one wanted.

I was in no rush to go inside to find out we were getting bounced, so we pulled the trading cart to the shed behind Grauntie's house. She rarely left the house and had no use for the shed, so we took it over when we moved in.

Daniel Boone went right on my family tree when I first created the trading cart. He traded furs when he was young. All his trading blazed the Wilderness Road through the Appalachian Mountains, right here in North Carolina, through Tennessee and into Kentucky. Thousands of people followed that trail—they were able to settle in Kentucky thanks to that road. How could I not be related to Daniel Boone after creating my trading cart? And he'd been in this very area—trading! I hadn't blazed a trail yet, but I did know what people wanted and made trades for what we needed. Boone genes were in my blood for sure. I closed my eyes and reminded myself, *I am the descendant of a great American pioneer.*

After we unloaded our stuff in the shed, Parker got busy organizing it all, placing the posters with the paper goods and the paints with the art supplies. He set the four plants on the ground outside the shed and stacked the books on the floor inside. Parker loved putting similar things in piles or boxes or bags. Along with finding missing things, being a top-notch organizer was one of his talents. That and smelling things no one else could. A human hound dog, you could say.

Maybe it was a waste to do all this organizing if we weren't even going to be here tomorrow, but we had a load of perfectly good stuff that had to be put away. Maybe Carly and Chase would take it over if we left.

Parker looked up at Grauntie's house. It was a small, square house, dirty white paint peeling off it like a bad sunburn.

"Yeah, we should go see what she needs," I said. My heart started tap dancing, wondering if our stuff would be sitting by the front door.

We left the wagons by the shed, then went inside. There was no sign of our things packed up in the living room. I dashed to my bedroom to see if a bag was in there, but everything was still stacked on the bed. I blew out a long breath.

I went back to the living room, where I suddenly noticed Grauntie was asleep in front of the TV, the side of her face pressed against the high, curved arm of her pale-blue couch. It seemed just as faded and worn as Grauntie—she almost blended in with it. Threads were pulled loose on the arms from long-ago cats that'd scratched it. I sure wished she still had cats. I would've liked the company of a warm, furry friend when I lay awake in bed, staring at the ceiling.

24

The room was so quiet that Grauntie's snores filled the whole space. I cleared my throat. "We're home. Any chores for us today?"

Grauntie's eyes fluttered open. "Who's there?" Her gaze darted around the room.

"It's us. Parker and Penny." Sometimes Grauntie forgot we were living with her, especially when she first woke up.

She nodded and blinked. "Yes, of course. Where's my pocketbook?"

"Right on your lap," I told her.

She patted her purse and smacked her lips a few times. "I could use a glass of water, Lucky Penny."

I gritted my teeth. Grauntie knew I hated being called Lucky Penny. Though she might've forgotten. She remembered stuff from long ago better than newer things. Maybe those things stuck to her mind better, having been there so long.

But how could anyone think I was lucky? The more I protested the nickname, the more people insisted on using it. In one school, kids on the bus even threw pennies at me. At another, two boys in back of the bus lifted me in the air like they were going to flip a coin—the coin being me.

Parker had gotten real upset when he saw what was happening, so I'd started screaming and kicking to set myself free. Then Parker and me got kicked off the bus, and shipped off from Uncle Dean's house, since he couldn't drive us to school and it was too far to walk. That's how we ended up here at Grauntie's.

"Don't call me Lucky Penny," I said to Grauntie, but she acted like she hadn't heard me.

Parker showed up with a glass of water. Grauntie drank it down in a long, loud slurp. "We need something for dinner. Had something planned out, can't remember what," she said. "Oh, and the screen door isn't latching when you kids leave for school in the morning. The cat keeps getting out."

No need reminding her we didn't have a cat. "We can take care of that," I said. "Anything else?"

"Some of Jenny Gray's strawberry jam would be nice for my . . . my bread in the morning. The crispy bread. I'm all out." She was rubbing her hands together, like she was worried.

"Okay. We'll be back in a few hours with dinner and jam and someone to fix the door." When we first came to Grauntie's, she still took care of most things. But lately, we'd had to take over and keep things running smoothly.

If not, she might decide taking care of us was too hard, and send us away.

I didn't mind the work. Besides, there wasn't much else to do, besides watch her boring programs and go through the old children's encyclopedias stacked on a bookshelf in the family room. I'd read them all twice. They were so old they said man was hoping to reach the moon one day. Maybe some of the books from Mr. Hanes would be interesting; it wouldn't take much to improve life at Grauntie's. But at least it didn't seem like she had plans to kick us out.

Unless she'd forgotten.

CHAPTER 4

If we weren't getting bounced yet, I had time to get New Hope back on the map and keep us there. Course, I had no idea how, so I'd be asking some questions when we went into town with our trading cart.

I went out to the shed to get ready, and Parker followed. "What should we bring today?" I asked him. We had a shed full of other people's castoffs, things we'd picked up along the roadside on garbage days. We took anything people didn't want. Couldn't bear to see perfectly good things thrown away. Things someone had once needed or loved. Anyway, you never know what will come in handy.

Somehow, Parker always knew exactly what people wanted to trade for. Stuff they didn't know was missing from their life. "Bring tin can critters." He looked around the dim space and pointed to a tall vase. "And the silverware, too." Parker put two plants in the back wagon, and he nodded at me that he was ready to go.

I set a few more things in there, just so people would have a chance to do some browsing.

Parker slipped on his gloves before grabbing the wagon handle. Sometimes an odor set him off into a fit when the world became too much. He'd cry and kick, and he'd hold his hands over his ears—probably so he didn't have to listen to himself. It was hard to calm him down. Rubbing the silky strip of his old baby blanket along his arms helped. Other times, I had to hold him tight until he stopped. Luckily, it didn't happen that often.

We walked down the dusty road toward town. Our first stop was Jenny Gray's. She was an easy trade 'cause she always made too much jam and was eager to get rid of it. I always knew when Jenny had made a new batch, 'cause she'd be filled up with color. We pulled the wagon up to her porch, then rapped on the door. "Parker and Penny's trading cart here to do business," I said.

No answer. But that wasn't surprising. Most folks in New Hope had no use for visitors and little enthusiasm for opening the door.

I pressed the doorbell a few times. "Trading cart's here. We've got just what you need."

After a few moments, Jenny appeared at the door. "Hello." She must've been inspired by her name, because everything she wore was gray: gray pants, gray shirt, gray shawl wrapped tightly around her. It was a very pale gray today. Guess she hadn't been making jam lately.

"Grauntie needs a few jars of jam, and we've got plenty to trade, all in the cart."

Jenny's eyes darted around like she was making sure it was okay to come out. Then she shuffled down her steps to look in the cart. She picked up the vase, but her eyes kept coming back to the plants. She rubbed one of the velvety green leaves between her fingers. "I haven't had a houseplant in years. And this is a lovely one." She picked it up, holding it against her. "This would be fine for a trade, if it's okay with you."

I smiled at Parker. He'd been right to bring the plants. "Sounds good."

"I'll get some jam." She took the plant inside and returned with three jars.

We waved goodbye to Jenny, then headed toward the center of town. "Mr. Gaiser should be able to fix the screen door. Plus, he's got all the parts at his store." I took the handle from Parker and pulled the cart.

New Hope's Finest loomed over us as we went into town. The boarded-up windows had big black X's painted across them. It felt like the building's wide eyes were watching us as we walked along, daring us to look up at it without feeling bad. The trees rustled even though there was no breeze. A flock of birds flew off the roof like a burst of wind. Some people thought the place was haunted. Others said it was cursed. You got a certain feeling walking by it, that was for sure. I studied my feet as we made our way past.

Main Street was quiet, just a car or two driving by. A few black-and-white-sketch people quietly walked down the street.

Parker stuck his nose in the air. "The Carlsons made meatloaf today."

"We'll get there in a bit," I said.

"I'm hungry now," Parker whined.

I sighed. "If you can be patient and wait, you can ask for dessert, too."

His smile returned, and we pulled the cart into the hardware store. Mr. Gaiser was hunched over on his stool, watching a show on a little TV behind the counter. Sitting like that, he looked even older than he was. "Fifty-nine and feeling fine," he liked to say. He always wore a flannel shirt, even in the summertime.

"Parker and Penny's trading cart, here to do business," I announced.

"Ah, my favorite young entrepreneurs." Mr. Gaiser's

color returned a bit when we visited. "And my first customers of the day. If business doesn't pick up one of these days . . ." He sighed. "What can I do for you?"

"Grauntie says the screen door isn't latching and needs to be fixed. We were hoping you could do that in exchange for something from the cart."

"Of course. Now, let me see what you have." Mr. Gaiser took a long time deciding, probably because he didn't have much else to do. First he picked up the plant and set it next to his register, then shook his head and put it back. He considered a few more things before he finally chose the vase. "I can stick my complimentary paint stirrers in here." He set it on the counter. "I'll stop by after supper tonight to fix the door."

"Thanks, Mr. Gaiser," I said. "Just be sure you don't go inside and disturb her. She might be sleeping." But that wasn't the whole truth. I just didn't want him to see how forgetful she'd become. We didn't need busybodies nosing around in our business.

"No problem," Mr. Gaiser said with a nod.

"Your car keys are under the order forms by the paint desk," Parker told him.

Mr. Gaiser dashed to look and he came back holding

his keys. His eyebrows popped up sky-high. "Now how did you know that? I looked everywhere for them."

Parker shrugged.

Mr. Gaiser shook his head, smiling. "Wish I had that kind of talent. You sure are something else."

Parker beamed.

Mr. Gaiser snapped his fingers. "Oh, almost forgot. I've got a few cans of mistake-paint for you and some rusty bolts. It'd be real helpful if you could take them off my hands." Mr. Gaiser shuffled off, adding them to our cart when he returned.

"Thanks!" I was already imagining those bolts as arms and legs on critters.

"Now we just need dinner," I told Parker, as we left the hardware store and headed for the diner. I knew what the Carlsons would pick from my cart. They couldn't resist my one-of-a-kind tin can creatures. Said it was half the reason people kept coming to their restaurant to eat.

I pulled the wagon into the diner. Suppertime was still a ways off, so only a few people sat sipping coffee at the counter. The more people there were in the diner, the more color all the customers had, like the glow bounced between them, growing bigger and bigger. Today, with only a few, it was just shades of gray in there. Jenny would've fit right in.

"Hello, Mr. Carlson," I said when he looked up. "We were hoping to make a trade for three of your specials tonight."

Parker pushed his sunglasses onto his head for a better look at the pies in the rotating counter display. He licked his lips as the slices slowly spun around under the shiny glass dome. If Parker were a superhero, his weakness would be sweets.

"Meatloaf tonight." Mr. Carlson rubbed his hands together as he came over from behind the counter. His skin was dark and shiny, and his eyes always seemed to glow like he was full of excitement. "Betty, come on out, dear!" he called to his wife. "The kids are here with new tin can critters."

When I first created the critters, I put Levi Strauss on my family tree, because he invented something special, too. He moved out to California during the gold rush to sell supplies to the miners, and worked with a customer to invent durable pants—blue jeans. Levi's. And people are still wearing them today. Maybe someday, my tin can critters will be just as famous. Would people call them Penny's Critters? I smiled, thinking, *I'm the descendant of a great inventor.*

Mrs. Carlson dusted flour off her hands, making a white cloud as she bustled out from the kitchen. "What did you bring me today?" A mist of flour settled in her curly, black hair, making it look gray.

The Carlsons were never drained dry of color. They were always steady in the middle. But when Parker and I showed up? They blazed full color.

I held up the little creature I'd constructed out of odds and ends. "It's a dog." His body was an old mint tin. Drawer handles underneath made his legs, and I had glued on a spring for his tail. His head was a small, round saltshaker, with washers for eyes and tiny keys for ears.

Mrs. Carlson took him from me and examined him. "Will you look at that?"

Mrs. Carlson's eyes were shiny as she stared at me. She had a daughter, Mary, who'd died ten years ago. Right after The Great Disappointment. Mary had been our age when she passed. Mrs. Carlson had never told me much more than that. I figured we were the ones stirring up her tears. One slipped down her cheek, shining on her dark skin like a star in the night sky.

Everyone was quiet for a moment until Mr. Carlson said, "You're quite the artist, Penny." He took the dog from Mrs. Carlson and looked it over. "Reminds me of our old dog, Charlie."

Mrs. Carlson blinked a few times, and the mistiness disappeared from her eyes. "You're right. Loved that fella. I swear, in my forty-five years I've had dozens of pets, but none like that dog. We'll name this critter Charlie."

"Perfect." Mr. Carlson set it on one of the shelves he'd installed on the back wall facing the counter. It was right next to the old, framed newspaper article about the Carlsons being the first black business owners in the county, so I knew that shelf was special to him. Dozens of our critters were up there. Mr. Carlson told me people came in every day to look at them, sipping their coffee and buying an extra pastry to enjoy while browsing. "A good investment," he called them.

After he added the dog to his display, he looked in our cart again and picked up the last plant. "I've got just the spot for this, right over by that lonely window. What if I gave you three more dinners, your choice? Then you won't need to worry about supper for tomorrow."

Parker smiled and nodded.

"Sounds good," I said. "Parker and I would like your lasagna, if you have it. I know Grauntie would like your chicken pot pie."

"And maybe a slice of apple pie?" Parker closed his eyes and smiled. He clearly didn't mind the smells in the diner.

"Certainly. Give me fifteen minutes and I'll have everything ready for you," Mrs. Carlson said, heading behind the counter. "I've got some empty jars and cans I need to get rid of. And of course, loads of bottle caps."

"We can take them for you," I said.

Parker sat down, but I pulled him back up. "We have one more place to go."

He squinted at me, confused.

"You'll see," I told him. "Be right back!" I shouted to the Carlsons.

We walked down the street to the town hall. Parker cocked his head.

"We're not trading. We're getting information. Stay here with the cart, okay?"

He nodded and I went inside the cool, air-conditioned building and walked up to the desk. "I need to see the mayor, please."

"What is your name?" the lady sitting there asked. The metal nameplate on her desk said MRS. NANCY TUTTLE, SECRETARY.

"Penny Porter," I answered. "I have an invitation to

stop by any time I have questions." Miss Meriwether had visited our school last year, and I'd been the only one to ask questions, so she had told me to stop by her office if I had more. This was a perfect time to take her up on it.

"Is she expecting you? She's about to leave town for a conference."

"I just have a few quick questions."

Mrs. Tuttle pursed her lips. "One moment." She picked up the phone and turned her back to me, murmuring into the receiver. When she hung up, she told me to go back to the mayor's office.

Miss Meriwether was the tallest woman I'd ever seen. She was sitting at her desk, but you'd swear she was standing behind it. "Come in," she said when I rapped on her open door.

Miss Meriwether usually had a bit of color to her, no matter how gloomy the day or her mood. But the corners of her mouth were always turned down, and I wasn't sure if she could smile if she wanted to. She wore her long, brown hair pulled back in a clip, like she didn't trust it not to fly around on its own.

"Take a seat, Penny. What's on your mind?" she asked.

I cleared my throat. "It has come to my attention that New Hope is not on the North Carolina map."

Somehow the corners of her mouth turned down even more. "I'm aware of that. There's no reason for people to come here in particular. So why would we be on the map?" She folded her long fingers in front of her.

I bounced one leg up and down. "I was thinking maybe if it was on the map, people would stop by. People would stay." Like me and Parker.

"We haven't been on the map since the year New Hope's Finest was set to open. I don't see us getting back on it."

I sat up straight. "Wait—we were on the map before?"

She nodded. "Years ago, when the orphanage was still operating, we were on the map. We expected a lot of traffic when the Finest was getting shaped up. But, well, you know what happened." Her color was draining.

I pressed my lips together. "I don't know all of it."

Miss Meriwether sighed. Then she was quiet. I thought maybe she wasn't going to tell me anything, but then she began. "Right after the orphanage closed . . . well, there was a lot of sadness." Her shoulders slumped. "Town officials thought it would be best to do something with that building. Make new memories. So we put out a call for proposals."

"That was a good idea." I tried to sound encouraging.

"We got a few suggestions, and the group we chose

promised to open the most fantastic, glorious attraction. One that would bring people to New Hope from miles around. But they didn't have enough cash to do it. So they asked the townspeople to pitch in and invest in the business. Everyone would get a share of the profits."

I gripped my seat. "I didn't know that."

"They'd started some renovations, but then that"— she lowered her voice to a whisper—"*doom painting* showed up." She sighed, and started talking normally again. "The investors took off with all the money," she said. "And that's that."

I scrunched my eyebrows together, thinking. "What was it going to be? The most amazing attraction ever? New Hope's Finest what?"

The mayor looked out the window and her normally gruff voice softened. "It was going to be a magnificent ballroom for dancing."

I paused. That was not the answer I had been expecting. That wouldn't even have been in my top one hundred guesses. "Really?"

She nodded. "New Hope's Finest Ballroom. People would come from across the state just to say they'd danced in North Carolina's grandest ballroom. Oh, people in this town had plans. Back then Mr. Tyler's gas station was open and ready for business. Mr. Carlson expanded the diner to accommodate all those hungry dancers. The five-and-dime loaded up on new stock. Mr. Kenney doubled the size of his market. Delores Owens converted her home into a bed-and-breakfast so travelers would have a place to stay. So many dreams were tied up in New Hope's Finest. And when it died . . ."

The town died, too, I thought. "Why didn't someone else open it?"

"No one had the money. And who'd want it now? People dump their trash behind the fence. It's overgrown with weeds. It's nothing now. Nothing but a waste."

"What if someone fixed it up?"

She crossed her arms. "And who's going to do that?"

I shrugged. "I could try."

The mayor laughed. "What an idea! Yes, Penny. You fix it up, and call me when you have a buyer."

That idea rippled through my brain. Fix up New Hope's Finest? Of course! That was the perfect way to get New Hope back on the map. The idea pounded my head and pulsed through my veins. "Thank you, ma'am!" I called, and I dashed out the door without looking back.

CHAPTER 5

Outside, I found Parker standing with the cart, holding a ten dollar bill. I looked in the cart. The forks and spoons were missing. "You sold the silverware?"

He nodded.

I twirled around. "Excellent! Because we're going to fix up New Hope's Finest, and someone will reopen it, and we're going to get New Hope back on the map! That ten dollars will help buy something we'll need for The Finest. Let's get our food. Then we need to start working. I knew we'd find a way!"

We hurried to the diner, where Mr. Carlson threw a bunch of dinner rolls and foil packets of butter in with our order.

"You children need anything else?" Mrs. Carlson asked.

"No, ma'am. We're fine," I said.

She held her arms open and smiled. "Come here, you two."

I walked over with my hands at my sides, stiffening as she hugged me. I always did. Otherwise, I might let myself fall into one of her hugs forever, feeling her soft hands gently pat my back. Smelling the flavors of the day mingled in the collar of her dress, along with that flowery perfume she wore. She was a small lady, but her hugs were huge. If I fell into a hug like that, I'd never want to come out. And I'd miss it like heck if we had to leave New Hope. No, I couldn't let one of her hugs into my heart. My heart lived inside one of those big wooden crates you'd need a crowbar to open. It was safe in there.

I pulled away before she did.

She looked at me for a moment, and her smile dimmed, then turned to Parker, who loved being hugged. When he finally let go of Mrs. Carlson, we waved goodbye and started lugging the cart back home. We said nothing as we walked, but Parker smiled the whole way, still soaking up all those cozy hug feelings. Later, that good feeling would be gone. I'd rather not have it at all than feel it slip away. The bad feeling of the missing-it part would outweigh the goodness of the having-it part. No, thanks.

We parked our cart, grabbed our things, and trudged up the driveway. "We're home!" I hollered as we walked in. Grauntie was right about the door; the screen bounced a few times when I slammed it behind me. I gave her the jars of jam, and Parker set out our dinners.

"Good work, kids." Grauntie nodded, her bottom lip jutting out like it usually did. She stood and smoothed her flowered housecoat. I wasn't sure if she wore the same one every day, or if she had several of the same pattern in her closet. We weren't allowed in her room. "It's important to pull your share of the load around here. Things are getting tougher for me."

"We know," I said.

"Your Uncle Jake hasn't been able to work for a while. Money's tight," Grauntie said.

I didn't remind her that Great-Uncle Jake hadn't been working because he was dead. Tried that once, and it'd just upset her.

We took our food onto the back porch and ate in silence. The Carlsons' meatloaf was so good, I didn't want to talk and distract myself from the flavors exploding in my mouth. The sun was still sleeping behind the clouds, getting ready to turn the show over to the moon in a few hours. The moon always looked especially big and lonely when you were gazing up at it in New Hope.

When we finished eating, I didn't run right off like usual. I had questions for Grauntie. "Did you know New

Hope's Finest was going to be a great big ballroom for dancing?" Grauntie wadded up her napkin and tossed it on the picnic table. "No, it was going to be an incredible snow globe display."

"That's weird," Parker said. "Who'd want to see that?"

"Why, everyone would," Grauntie said.

I scrunched my eyebrows together, thinking that was even more unlikely than a ballroom. "Was it supposed to be both things? Snow globes and dancing? Seems like they'd get broken with all that twirling around."

"There was never going to be dancing. People from across North Carolina were going to come to the biggest display of snow globes in the state. No, in the country!" Grauntie's color flushed as she talked about it.

Even though we couldn't go in her bedroom, when I passed by I could see that she had a big display case filled with snow globes.

"New Hope's Finest Snow Globe Emporium." When she said it, she sounded fifty years younger. She sighed and rubbed at a splotch of gravy on her housecoat.

I said nothing else, 'cause I didn't want to ruin her good mood. I cleaned up our takeout boxes and wiped them out to add to our stash in the shed. Parker washed the glasses and silverware while I dried. Then we went outside to work.

We saw Mr. Gaiser pull into the driveway and waved to him. He waved back and headed for the front door.

I went inside the shed, meaning to clean it up, but my fingers started wiggling, tapping the workbench faster and faster. An idea was making its way down from my brain. I had no choice but to let my hands do their work. I'd always enjoyed making things, but ever since we'd moved to New Hope, ideas flowed out of me like a waterfall. That's another reason I liked the town so much. It just felt like I belonged there. "Parker, I need your help."

"Critters?" he called from outside.

"Yep." I grabbed a bunch of tin cans we'd gotten at the diner and peeled off the labels. I snatched up the ones that seemed to be wiggling and wobbling. Sometimes the things I needed for my pieces hummed. I don't know how they talked to me, but they did.

Parker rummaged through the odds and ends box and pulled out all sorts of castoffs: screws and old springs, broken watches and rusty keys. He dumped everything on the workbench.

Silently, we laid out the parts with the cans, looking for the best creature combinations. Parker found a few old spice tins that we mounted on the cans as heads.

A pair of keys would make nice arms.

"Look!" Parker set a napkin ring on one of the heads like a crown.

I crossed my arms, stepping back to see the effect, and nodded. "Everybody's going to want that one."

We used bottle caps and buttons for eyes, and an old metal scrub pad for hair. Soon, three critters were lined up and ready for glue. "You best get out of here, now. I'll be up to the house soon."

Parker dashed out of the shed. He hated the smell of the glue. But it was the best thing to use. Waterproof, fireproof, weatherproof. Strong enough to keep everything together forever. Too bad more things weren't like that. Too bad you couldn't use it on families.

Once everything was glued together, I shut off the light and stepped outside. It was dark, and the trees were rustling in the wind, telling secrets I longed to know. I stared up at the moon, just a bright smidge of light way up high. Something big and wonderful had to be waiting beyond that crack in the sky, if only I could crawl through. That must be where all the wonder in the universe was stored.

I loved looking up at the moon so much, I was certain that somehow, some way, I was related to Neil Armstrong.

He was the first man to walk on the moon. It was like a little part of me had been there once. Yep, he was on my family tree, too. *I am the descendant of a space explorer.*

The idea made me so happy. But sometimes I felt so small, so unimportant, gazing up at it all. It was times like that I really wished I had a family. I'd feel a lot less helpless looking up at all those stars while sitting on my mama's lap, with her arms tucked around me like a safety harness bolting me to the earth.

Or maybe she wouldn't want to look at the stars. Mama said not to hope for too much, but did she ever have any big dreams? I'd give anything to know more about my family. More about who I am. Was my father a hard worker? Did he do great things, like the people on my family tree? Was he related to notable people? Or maybe he was a notable person, too. I crossed my fingers and hoped that someday I'd find out who he was and what amazing things he'd done.

Getting a town back on the map would be pretty amazing, if I could do it. *Neil Armstrong made it to the moon*, I thought. Fixing up the Finest was practically no work at all.

I pulled Mama's letter out of my pocket and reread it to make sure I wasn't breaking any of her rules by trying to fix up the Finest. The moon was bright enough for me to read by.

Dear Penny,

I'm sorry I won't be there to take care of you and Parker. You'll have to be extra strong now, and look out for your brother. Sometimes, the world is just too much for him. I suppose since you were born five minutes before him that means you'll always be in charge. Sorry about that. Life's not fair, best you know that now.

I've managed to learn quite a few other things in my short time here, and I'm going to share those truths with you, so you won't get hurt learning them on your own like I did:

#1: Don't expect too much from the world. That way, you'll never be disappointed.

#2: Don't ask for help. We're not a charity case.

#3: You should never, ever have to ask someone to love you. I left my mama in charge of you two for now. My family promised to always take care of you when I'm gone, so you won't have to go into the system.

Know that I'll always, always, always love you two.

Mama

I folded up the letter. Seemed like my plan was okay. I wasn't going to ask anyone for help, not without offering a trade or something in return. I suppose if someone offered to help, that would be okay, since I wouldn't be asking.

I could do this.

I trudged up to the house, tired from the day. Before bed, I pulled out the family tree sheet from the drawer in my nightstand and studied it. I'd drawn the tree myself. The trunk was a little too wide at the bottom, and the branches were too straight to look real. Mama's side only had a couple spindly branches on it, holding the few names of people I knew, mostly folks we had stayed with. I hadn't bothered adding Nanny Gladys. She didn't deserve a spot. The rest of Mama's people probably didn't belong there, either. They hadn't wanted us. They didn't keep us. Isn't that what family's supposed to do?

But Daddy's side was wonderful. It had lots of long, thick branches from top to bottom: Martin Luther King, Jr., the famous civil rights leader; Pocahontas, the Powhatan Indian woman who saved John Smith;

Harriet Tubman, one of the leaders of the Underground Railroad; Gandhi, the peaceful protestor from India; and more. Most of the names came from the *Notable People* book. Grauntie's encyclopedias had helped me choose other people, too.

I grabbed the blue pen I used whenever I added a name and wrote "Sacagawea" on a new branch that I squeezed in between Rosa Parks and Thomas Edison. After tracing my finger over each name, I put the paper back in the nightstand. Then I pulled out a notebook that still had some pages left in it. I had to write a letter to the map company.

Dear person in charge of deciding which towns get put on the map,
My name is Penny Porter, and I live in New Hope, NC, which sadly has not been included on your map for years, not since New Hope's Finest was set to open but didn't. I think it's important that you know we are fixing it up now and it'll be open real soon, and since many people will want to come here, you should definitely put New Hope back on the map.

Can you please write back and let me know when your new map comes out and if New Hope will be included? It's real important. More important than you know. Please write back ASAP!

Sincerely,
Penny Porter

I wrote the address on an envelope, folded the letter, and slid it inside. I fished a stamp out of Grauntie's desk in the living room, stuck it on the envelope, and dropped it in the mailbox.

Before going back inside, I looked up at the moon again. "Please let this work," I whispered, hoping my wish would wiggle through that bright slice of sky to the part of the universe that made good things happen.

CHAPTER 6

Project Fix Up New Hope's Finest was almost officially under way the next morning—but first, Grauntie had a chore list waiting for us on the kitchen table. Her writing was getting harder to read, and sometimes the things she wrote down didn't make sense. But today she wanted us to feed the cat (that we didn't have), clean the kitchen, and sweep the deck. I woke Parker, and we zipped through our work, then headed out with our trading cart.

Glenda from the Lovin' Oven took a plant in exchange for donuts and gave us bottles of water, too. Then, we walked to Chase's house. I banged on his door. "Chase, come out. We've got an adventure lined up."

No answer.

When Parker and I explored the woods or went junk picking, Chase always called it boring. He was the most bored person I ever knew. Yawned all the time. I'm not even sure what would make him excited. I banged the knocker again. "Come on, you're going to like this."

Still nothing.

"Think maybe he finally died of boredom?" Parker asked.

"No, he's probably just drained dry of color."

"We've got donuts!" Parker shouted, clutching the box against his chest.

The door opened. "What kind?" Chase asked, his eyes half-closed.

"The best kind, glazed. And you can have one as payment when you come with us," I said.

He looked at the box, shrugged, and stuck his thumbs under his overall straps. It was hot enough already that he hadn't bothered wearing a shirt underneath.

Next we stopped at Carly's and found her sitting on the front porch, staring at something I couldn't see. "Hey," I said.

"Hey." Her feet hung off the porch swing, but she wasn't kicking them back and forth like I would've been if I were sitting on a swing. How anyone could sit perfectly still on a swing was beyond me.

"We've got the biggest adventure ever planned, and donuts, too," I announced. "Wanna come?"

Carly shrugged and slipped off the swing. "'Kay," she said, like I was suggesting we scrub week-old dirty dishes instead of taking on the most exciting project any of us had ever tried. "I'm going with Penny and Parker," she hollered inside to her mother.

"All right," called her mama softly. Apparently, Carly's daddy left New Hope after The Great Disappointment, even though her mama had just delivered Carly. Her mama left the door unlocked all the time, so he could get in if he ever returned. *Maybe if New Hope gets on the map he'll find his way back*, I thought. Getting back on the map might help more people than just me and Parker. And that would be a good thing, because it felt a little selfish doing this only for us.

No one said much as we headed down the street toward town. Birds chirped and cicadas buzzed, which reminded me how quiet New Hope really was. The asphalt stretched ahead of us, hot, dusty, and empty. No cars zoomed past. No one here had anywhere to go that was important enough to require zooming.

"When do I get that donut?" Chase asked.

"When we get to our destination," I explained.

"Which is?" Carly asked.

"The biggest, best thing we will ever do."

"Doubt that," Chase said.

"Penny, I won't be any help," Carly said. "I'm not good at anything."

"Now that's just not true," I said. "Wait till we get there. You'll be so excited."

No one said anything. I'd heard enthusiasm was contagious, but not in New Hope. We tramped along until we got onto Main Street and stood in front of New Hope's Finest. I parked our cart and spread my arms wide. "Here we are."

Chase looked around, his big blue eyes narrowing. "I don't understand."

"I've got permission to fix up New Hope's Finest so a new buyer will open it and we can get New Hope back on the map," I explained.

"Fix New Hope's Finest?" Chase repeated. "Boring."

"Oh! It was going to be a giant playground." Carly stared at the building looming over us. Blinking, she bit her lower lip, and her color bloomed. Carly's hair was a beautiful chestnut brown when she was in full color.

I didn't want to see her color drain, so I didn't mention that the mayor said it was going to be a ballroom and Grauntie said it was meant to be a snow globe display. "Let's go see," I said. We ducked under the chain roping off the gravel road that led to the entrance. It was a hike up the hill. When we got to it, the fence was higher than our heads. I gulped, imagining what might be back there.

The padlock lay on the ground, so the gate was easy to open—I just had to slide the latch to the right and then swing open the two big wooden doors. The sun slipped from behind a cloud, like it finally wanted to watch what we were doing. But it blinded us, and for a moment we couldn't see anything.

When it went away and everything came into focus, we were speechless.

"Oh. Wow," Parker finally said, looking around.

Chase groaned, and Carly sighed.

"Can you believe this?" I shouted. "It's amazing!"

"Amazingly horrible," Chase moaned. "You said this was going to be fun."

I shot a nasty look at him. "It will be. It's like a giant trading shed. Look at all these treasures!" I spun around, taking everything in: mounds of old tires, boxes of junk spilling over, old bicycles, busted TVs, and even a car—a rusty old VW bug. A feeling like electricity tingled through me, filling my head with dozens of ideas.

"Penny, there's too much!" Chase groaned.

Apparently Chase had forgotten about my talent for finding homes for castoffs.

"We're supposed to clean all this up?" Carly asked.

"Ugh. Why?" Chase asked. "How?"

"I don't know. Give it away? Sell it? Make stuff out of it?" I closed my eyes and stuck my arms out, letting the current of ideas flow through me. I popped one eye open. "Don't you feel it?"

The three of them shook their heads. "Feel what?" Parker asked.

"Excitement. Energy. Ideas!" I hollered. "Close your eyes and hold out your arms."

They did, so I closed mine again, too. "What do you feel?"

"Depressed," Chase said.

"I feel tired," Carly said.

With a sigh, I opened my eyes.

Carly and Chase plopped onto their bottoms. I walked over and pulled them both up again. "We can do this!"

"It's a dumb idea. We can't fix this up," Chase said. "No one can. Let's go home."

I closed my eyes and pictured my family tree. Who could help me right now? I snapped my fingers. "Doctor

Carlos Juan Finlay." I had known he'd come in handy someday.

"Huh?" Carly said.

"He was a doctor from Cuba who believed this horrible disease, yellow fever, was transmitted by mosquitoes. But no one believed him. They teased him and called him the Mosquito Man. It took twenty years for him to prove he was right. He's on my family tree, so I've got some of his perseverance in me. No matter what anyone says, or what mean names they might call me, I'm going to make this happen." Pride swelled in me. *I am the descendant of a famous researcher.*

"It'll probably take *us* twenty years, too," Chase said.

"How do you know he's on our family tree?" Parker asked.

"Just a hunch." *It's possible our daddy was Cuban.* I wondered if Dr. Finlay had had a case of the freckles like me. Too bad he hadn't found a cure for that.

Parker shrugged and started organizing things into piles.

I walked up to the building. It was three stories high and made of brick, with ivy growing up the side of it. It was the size of three or four big houses. Boards were nailed over the windows. The giant metal front door must've looked awfully scary to the orphans when they first came here. The rusty iron fences that stood on both sides of the building had probably protected vegetable gardens once—though the little patches of ground behind them now held nothing but weeds. A gust of wind swirled past us, and the building seemed to moan. No wonder some people said it was haunted. "Let's check it out, guys."

Carly and Chase froze, and Parker stopped his work. Slowly, they joined me on the porch, where we stood in front of the door.

"What do you think is in there?" Chase asked. "You don't think there are really ghosts, do you?"

"Do you think there could be animals?" Carly asked.

"Or ghosts?" Chase asked again. "I hope there aren't ghosts."

I opened the door and peered inside. "Nothing's in here. It's totally empty."

We walked into the building. Our footsteps echoed in the hallway, which led to a set of stairs in the middle and big rooms on either side. There was no carpet and no furniture. Nothing but spiderwebs and dust. Parker coughed, then pinched his nose, but I didn't smell anything.

I did *feel* something, though, and it wasn't scary. It was exciting, like I'd been running and laughing. Like a party was about to start. My heart felt twice as big, and my fingers twitched with excitement. I looked at my feet to make sure I wasn't floating. How could an empty building have that effect on me?

We went through a doorway to another empty room in back. The walls looked gray, but I figured they must've been painted white once. We climbed a set of stairs and found a bunch of empty rooms. Another staircase led to a third floor with even more rooms, just like the ones on the second floor. As we explored, that weird feeling only got stronger.

"I bet there were going to be toy displays up here," Carly said. "In all the kids' old bedrooms."

"No way. My dad told me this was going to be a natural history museum, with dinosaurs and fossils and stuff," Chase said. "Probably each room was going to have a different animal in it."

"That's dumb. The rooms aren't big enough for dinosaurs," Carly said.

They kept arguing until I said, "Guys! It's nothing now, and it won't be until we fix it up. So let's get to work."

We went downstairs and opened the door to a basement.

"No way am I going down there," Chase said, scampering out the door with Carly and Parker on his heels.

I peered down the stairs. I couldn't see much, but there was a big empty room off to one side, and old equipment and boxes on the other. *No need to work down there, especially with no light*, I thought. I shut the door and went outside, the humidity hitting me like a wall after the coolness inside the building. "Let's get to it."

Parker, Chase, and Carly stood outside, waiting for me to tell them what to do. We started off rolling all the tires into one pile, then went through the boxes of junk and separated those into different sections, too: old tools, broken appliances, plastic stuff, and miscellaneous items.

A few hours later, we'd eaten all the donuts and drunk our water, but we were hungry from the hard work. A bathroom break would be nice, too, I figured. Wasn't sure the ones inside would work.

"Let's trade for some lunches," I said.

"And we all need work gloves," Chase said, looking at Parker's with big eyes.

"Come on!" I shouted, thrilled we were really doing it. We were fixing up the Finest. Everyone in town was going to be so excited.

CHAPTER 7

We stopped at the diner first. The sounds of clattering pots and pans came from the kitchen, drowning out the lively music on the radio.

"Penny, dear, are you all here for lunch?" Mrs. Carlson asked with a smile.

"Yep!" I pulled my trading cart to the counter. "I made a few new critters last night that I think you'll like."

She came over and set her hand on my shoulder. It felt nice. Too nice.

I stepped back.

She folded her hands in front of her. "Of course, we can trade if you like."

I nodded. "Excellent. See, we're busy cleaning up New Hope's Finest, and we got hungry—"

Mrs. Carlson's smile withered away. "What do you mean by 'Cleaning up New Hope's Finest'?"

"The mayor said I could, so we can get someone else to buy it and get New Hope back on the map."

Mrs. Carlson turned away from me. "That place is cursed," she whispered in a soft, sad voice. "Best you leave it alone, before something else bad happens."

"Cursed? Why? Did another terrible thing happen there, besides the investors leaving?"

She opened her mouth, then closed it, shaking her head.

I bit my lip. How could I explain to her that something bad would happen if I *didn't* fix the Finest up? That Parker and I would get bounced? It was too hard to explain. "But it's been sitting empty for so long. Someone's got to do something."

She wiped down the counter without looking at me. "We've been ignoring it for years. Don't see why that has to change. Now, what can I get you to eat?"

I couldn't look her in the eyes. "Just a turkey sandwich, thanks. Choose what you'd like from the cart in exchange."

I wandered outside to take another look at the Finest. It was just down the road from the diner. Sure, it was big and empty and old, but I couldn't believe this building could cause so many bad feelings. I didn't feel that way about it at all. I was still brimming with excitement about the whole thing. I went back inside, confused.

Once we were settled at the counter and eating our sandwiches, Mr. Carlson came out. "What's this I hear about you cleaning New Hope's Finest? That's not going to sit well with most folks."

"Why not?" I asked. "We're turning it into something new."

"People get set in their ways, get comfortable with the way things are. And that's a big undertaking for you kids." Mr. Carlson said the word "big" like it was a mile long. He clucked his tongue and shook his head. "What a shame it became a dumping ground, when it was supposed to be an art museum."

"I thought it was going to be a natural history museum," Chase said.

I set down my sandwich. "I'm hearing lots of different things about what it was going to be." I wanted New Hope's Finest to come back to life and make everyone full of hope again. Help them forget about those dumb doom paintings. How could a painting be the reason everything fell apart?

I cleared my throat. "Have any of you ever seen one of the doom paintings?"

Chase and Carly's nice colors faded as they shook their heads. Mr. Carlson rubbed his chin. "My neighbor got one a few years back. Lost his dog after that. Then his garage fell down." He looked off into the distance, shaking his head like he was right there in front of the ruined building. "No, most folks who get one hide it in the basement, or tuck it in the back of a closet. I think people would throw them out if Willy Brown hadn't crashed his pickup right after he tossed his in the garbage. People keep them, but they keep them out of sight. I've never seen one."

"Any idea what they look like?" I asked.

Mr. Carlson rubbed his chin. "From what I hear, they're confusing. Not a picture of anything, per se. Just a bunch of random paint strokes."

I tried to picture it in my mind. "Does he leave a note?"

"Nope. Just a painting, signed with his name. A few people have confronted him, demanding to know what they mean and why he left them, but he's never said." Mr. Carlson sighed. "Joe is a troubled man, after everything that's happened. Doesn't even answer his door. You rarely see him in town."

We finished lunch, and Mr. Carlson gave us more water bottles to take with us.

"Where's Mrs. Carlson?" I wasn't looking for a hug, certainly not. But it seemed like proper manners to say goodbye.

Mr. Carlson studied his shoes. "She went home to lie down."

I hadn't noticed her leaving. "Is she sick?" She had been okay when we came in.

"In a way, I suppose. Just missing Mary so much. Happens every so often. She just needs some time alone, and she'll be all right. Don't you worry." His eyes looked tired and sad.

Sometimes Mama would get like that, when she was alive. But I didn't like thinking about kind Mrs. Carlson getting so upset that she had to hurry home and be alone. "I'll make her a critter tonight to cheer her up. A free one, no trade needed."

Mr. Carlson smiled. "That would be very nice."

I waved goodbye, then we headed to the hardware store and asked Mr. Gaiser for gloves and bug spray on trade.

His eyebrows shot up when he heard that we were cleaning up the Finest. "Are you, now?"

I nodded. "We'll get it all cleaned up and find a new buyer. Mayor said I could."

"I hate to discourage you kids, but you're wasting your time." Mr. Gaiser handed me four pairs of work gloves and bug spray. He chose a few things from the cart.

I tried not to groan. Why wasn't anyone excited? "It's a perfectly good building. It shouldn't just be abandoned and neglected. It just needs someone to care for it."

"I think it's too late," he said. He leaned against his counter, staring out the front window. "The town sure did change once the orphanage shut down. Those kids might've been odd, but they brought life to the town."

"What do you mean, odd?" I asked.

"Don't know how to explain it, but they weren't like other kids." He shrugged. "It was so quiet 'round here when it closed. Then when we all thought New Hope's Finest would be bringing some life back to this place . . ." He whistled, shaking his head. "That building has brought so much sadness since, I doubt it could ever be something wonderful again." He was practically drained of color as he said the sad words.

I gritted my teeth, annoyed by all this doom-and-gloom talk. "We're sure going to try. Bye, Mr. Gaiser." I walked out the door.

"Don't listen to him. I think it could be wonderful again," Carly said when we got outside.

"Thanks, Carly," I said.

"I wonder why no one has cleaned it up before?" she asked.

"Because they were smart enough not to try," Chase said.

Chase may have been talking grumpy, but his color was getting deeper. At least a few people were excited about the project, even if they weren't willing to say so.

Back at the site, we tackled another corner filled with junk. Looking at it all in a big picture was overwhelming, but focusing on just one small spot made it easier. So we worked and laughed and joked, and the hours flew by. Even though the place was messy, just being there made us all feel good. I could tell by the way everyone's colors glowed.

"Why are there so many broken bicycles?" Carly asked, dragging a rusty one over to the bike pile.

I shrugged. "Why would anyone throw out an old box of records?" I held up a big black disc while my fingers itched and the idea of making wind chimes came back in my mind. I looked up at the tall trees and pictured a long string of records spinning in the breeze. I closed my eyes and saw tires stacked up in crazy sculptures, bicycle wheels connected to each other, climbing to the sky. The ideas were whizzing around my head so fast I had to sit down. I rubbed my temples, hoping to hold off the headache I felt coming on.

"You all right?" Parker asked.

I nodded. "Idea overload." I rubbed a finger over the grooves in the record.

"We'll have to come back tomorrow. It's getting close to suppertime," Chase said. "Can't be late."

We gathered our things and latched the gate behind us, then shuffled down the road toward home.

I couldn't yet explain the vision in my mind, but something big and grand was going to happen at New Hope's Finest. I knew it just as certain as I knew the sun would rise the next morning.

CHAPTER 8

After dinner, I made a special tin can critter for Mrs. Carlson. I used a tiny tin box and a dome-shaped bell Mr. Gaiser used to have on his counter to ring for service. He had traded it to me when the dinger broke, and it made a perfect head. Triangle picture hooks would work for the ears, two marbles for the eyes, and a few chunky screws made perfect legs. I cut up an old guitar string for whiskers. Then all I needed was a tail. I found an old extension cord and cut off the end. Mrs. Carlson was going to love it.

Tired from the day, I brought the critter to my room and flopped onto my bed. The room was still pink and decorated with ballerinas from when Gert lived in it as a kid. I had never asked Grauntie if I could add my own decorations to the room because I knew what her answer would be: no. No one had ever let me decorate just the way I wanted. Maybe that's why working on the Finest seemed like a treat instead of work.

I changed into my pajamas and started reading the *Great Americans* book I'd gotten from Mr. Hanes. Fixing up New Hope's Finest was nothing compared to what some of these people had done.

I'd fallen asleep with the book in my arms, and when I woke, my hand was stuck to the page about Jim Thorpe. I read a bit about him. He was a famous American Indian athlete in the 1920s who won Olympic gold medals in track and played professional football and baseball. The book said he was one of the greatest athletes ever.

I closed my eyes, wondering what it would be like to be so good at so many things. Imagine being related to someone like him. *Maybe I am*, I thought. The book said he was a twin, too! Twins run in families!

I read on and learned his twin brother died when he was nine. With a gulp, I slammed the book shut. I didn't even like thinking about such sadness. My heart would be totally empty without Parker. Even so, I jotted Jim

Thorpe's name onto my family tree. What a nice new addition. *I'm the descendant of a great athlete.*

I tiptoed out of my room. If it was another clear day, we could get right to work, so I quietly opened the front door for a peek at the weather. And what I saw made me freeze. I blinked several times, then swallowed a scream.

There was a painting on the front stoop. I closed my eyes and shook my head to clear it, like maybe I'd been seeing things, but, no, it was still there, a canvas of scribbles. I closed the door behind me and went out for a better look. Sure enough, it was signed by Joe C.—Joe Jinx! That scream was stuck in my throat like a fistful of dry crumbs.

Had my teacher been right? Mr. Hanes had said just talking about one would bring it to you. I picked up the painting. It was probably a foot and a half high, by two feet wide. It wasn't a picture of anything, so much as it was a bunch of swirls and squiggles. Seemed like the shape of something was hiding in all those whorls, but I couldn't work it out in my brain.

My hands shook as I remembered all the horrible things that happened to other people when they got a doom painting. What bad thing would happen to me? I gulped and squared my shoulders. I wasn't going to give up because of this. Or maybe, just maybe, the work we were doing at the Finest would create something so good it would overpower the doom painting?

I knew Grauntie shouldn't see it, though. She'd probably never come out of her bedroom again, she'd be so scared. I wasn't going to hide it in the house, either—I was going to take it back to the person who painted it.

I picked it up, holding it against my chest, and ran across the yard to hide the painting in the shed without looking at it again. Then I went in the house and poured bowls of cereal for me and Parker. Grauntie would be up soon. I tried to keep my hands from shaking while I poured milk over our cornflakes, but I still dribbled some onto the counter by mistake.

"Good morning, Lucky Penny. Can you make me coffee?" Grauntie asked me as she shuffled down the hall toward the couch.

"Sure." I reached for the can in the cupboard.

Parker sat down in front of his cereal and started eating, watching me as I got the coffee ready. He bit his lip when I overfilled the pot with water.

"We'll be exploring with Chase and Carly today. Need us to get anything while we're in town?" I asked Grauntie.

"Don't you have school?" she asked.

"It's summer break."

"Is it, now? All right then. Looks like you two can take it easy today. Have a break. I'll have a chore sheet for you tomorrow."

"Thanks, ma'am," I said.

Parker and I gulped down our cereal. I gave Grauntie her coffee, and then we were out the door.

"What's wrong?" Parker asked as I ran toward the shed.

"You'll see." I stopped in front of the shed. "Don't freak out."

Parker groaned. "Now I will."

I stepped into the shed and came out with the painting. "I found this on our front porch this morning."

Parker's jaw dropped. "Is that . . .?"

"I think so. It's signed by Joe C. And we're taking it back to him, 'cause we don't want it. We'll pick up Carly and Chase after, and get back to work up at New Hope's Finest. We've got to create something so amazing there, it cancels out the doom painting." What else could I do? Just sit around and wait for something bad to happen?

He nodded. "Makes sense. If you're not worried, I'm not worried."

Oh, man. I couldn't let him know I was actually a little worried. Whenever I got upset about something, he got upset.

I covered the painting with an old towel we had in the shed, then put it in the trading cart, along with the special critter for Mrs. Carlson. We took off, heading for the edge of town.

Walking along in silence, I tried to chase the bad thoughts out of my head. But they fluttered around anyway, like the time a pack of moths swarmed our trading shed. Could that painting mean something awful was going to happen with New Hope's Finest—*again*? Were we going to get hurt working there? Or maybe it was proof that Parker and I were going to get bounced somewhere soon.

I stopped walking and pressed my fingers against my temples, closing my eyes. "Getting back on the map is going to fix everything."

Parker shrugged. "If you say so."

We walked on until we came to a big house with pillars out front. The house probably had been bright white at one point, but now it was dingy, with overgrown trees covering the windows. Moss coated the roof, and most of the shutters hung crooked. If that house could speak, it would probably cry for help.

The driveway was filled with junk: a big paint-splattered ladder; a pickup truck with flat tires; some construction vehicles. Whatever business Joe Jinx used to be in, it sure didn't look like he was working in it anymore.

I tucked the painting under my arm and walked up the path leading to the front door. Grass grew between the bricks, and I had to watch my step because some of them were sticking up. I got to the door and rang the bell.

No one answered, so I rang it again. And again, this time pounding on the door, too. "Open up, Joe. I'm not leaving until you tell me why you left me this painting." I rang the bell three more times before the door opened. I stepped back.

A man stood there, his eyes fixed on the ground. He had puffy blond hair like a cloud around his face, and a matching beard. His skin was smooth, like he was young, but his eyes looked a thousand years old. "You found a painting this morning?" His voice was slow and deep, but soft.

I crossed my arms, but just looking at his slumped shoulders made it hard to keep feeling angry. "Yeah, on our Grauntie's front porch." I held the painting out to him. "Why did you leave it there?"

He shrugged. "Don't know."

"What do you mean, you don't know?"

"I paint them in my sleep. I never know where they end up." He scratched the back of his head.

"But what does it mean?" I snuck a look at the painting again.

He shrugged. "Bad luck, most people say."

I held it out to him. "I don't want it."

He looked at it. "What am I supposed to do with it?"

"You can paint over it. Paint something nice, while you're awake. I'm not even sure what this is supposed to be." I turned the canvas around and squinted at the painting, but couldn't make sense of it.

He shrugged, and sadness rushed my heart. "What's your name?" I asked.

"Joe Jinx."

I shook my head. "That's just what other people call you. What's your real name?"

He said nothing for a moment, then swallowed hard. "Joe Clark."

I set down the painting and stuck out my hand. "I'm Penny Porter, and, no, I'm not lucky, so don't say it. This is my twin brother, Parker."

Joe narrowed his eyes and looked at me. Really looked at me. He must've been studying my freckles. Probably trying to count them.

"I know. I got lots of freckles. Looks like a truck drove by and splattered me with mud. Looks like a dot-to-dot picture. Don't bother coming up with a joke. I've heard them all."

"Wasn't going to make a joke. I knew a kid with freckles like yours, that's all," Joe said. "His friends called him Wren, since his face was speckled like one of their eggs."

I paused, a good feeling swelling up in my heart. "Didn't think anyone else had a case of freckles like this." Except for my dad, if he'd been the one to give 'em to me.

"Where did you say you live?" he asked.

"With my great-aunt. Francine Parker."

He looked away, like he was watching something in the far, far distance.

I cleared my throat. "I've got an idea. We're cleaning up New Hope's Finest. The mayor said I could fix it up and find a buyer. Since you like painting, how about you paint inside the building instead of your . . . other paintings? I'm paying people with goods from my trading cart. I've got some good stuff to choose from."

He turned to me and pursed his lips. His eyes grew dark. "You shouldn't even be stepping foot in that place."

My eyes widened, surprised by his tone. "I already did, and it's going to be great."

"Don't go there." He shook his head. "You don't know what you're getting into."

A shiver raced through me, but I couldn't let his words scare me. We had to fix up the Finest. "Whatever we do, it's going to be better than it is now."

"Then that must be why I made you a painting. Something bad is going to happen if you work there. I beg you, stay away from the Finest." And with that, he walked back inside and slammed the door.

CHAPTER 9

Parker and I stood there for a moment, like Joe might come out again with an explanation, but he didn't.

"Why do we have to stay away?" I hollered. "What's going to happen?"

No answer.

Parker and I looked at each other, a nervous feeling bouncing back and forth between us. "Everything is going to be fine," I told Parker, and he smiled.

I left the painting on Joe's porch, and we headed off to pick up Carly and Chase. They were both sitting on Carly's front porch, waiting for us.

Carly swung her feet as she sat on the swing. She hopped off and hurried over with a backpack. "I brought a notebook so I can write down all the paint colors we have. And a marker to write the color on the can."

"Good thinking. You're in charge of that," I told her.

We dashed up the steep road to the Finest, and I

crossed my fingers that nothing would go wrong. But I couldn't stop thinking about Joe's warning.

We opened the gate and got to work. Carly went inside to make a list of the paint. Parker and Chase unloaded a big pile of boxes. I tried sorting through some old tools and scrap metal, but my fingers were jerking and twitching. I needed to create.

I sat down by the old records and grabbed a spool of fishing line someone had tossed back there with rods and lures. Those records were going to be part of a wind chime. A big one.

I looped the fishing wire between the holes in the records, leaving some of them closer together, some farther apart. I tied tiny jingle bells along the string in between each one. It was a good distraction from thinking about that darn painting.

I had seven strands by the time I was done, each one more than three times as long as I was tall. Then I tied them all onto a spare bicycle tire, and tied a big metal hook on top that I could loop over a tree limb.

The trees were so tall, I'd have to hunt down a ladder to hang my chime. I decided I'd find one in town and grab lunch, too.

My tummy grumbled at the very thought of food, so I

told Parker and Chase to clean up, then went inside to get Carly. I could hear her working in one of the back rooms. "Carly, we're going to get lunch." As I walked into the room she was working in, I blinked a few times. "What's this?"

Carly stood on a chair with a paintbrush, dabbing at the wall. She looked over her shoulder. "I was checking out the colors on the wall, and couldn't help myself. It was like something got a hold of my hand and made me start painting. Doesn't it look amazing?"

"Wow!" One wall was covered from floor to ceiling with splotches of color. The other wall had tiny paintings of animals and things, like a brown bear, a brown leaf, an orange carrot, a red apple. It was an incredible mural. "This will definitely help sell this building to someone. Who wouldn't love it?"

"I'm going to do the whole room like this." She hopped off her chair and wiped her hands on a rag. "I never knew I liked painting so much."

"We should save some paint to use upstairs." I grabbed a big bucket of it. The label said it was five gallons. It was heavy, so it would probably be enough to paint a few rooms.

"Penny, that's gotta be like fifty pounds. We need help with it," Carly said.

"I can do it." I shuffled a few feet with the can, then set it down. I did this again and again until I got to the bottom of the stairs. Then I set the can on a stair. And then the next. And the next. My arms shook from the weight of it.

But, finally, I had it on the top step. I sat down for a minute, tired from the hard work. And the can toppled over, yellow paint pouring down the stairs like a waterfall.

At the bottom of the stairs, Carly's jaw dropped open.

I closed my eyes for a minute. This wasn't going to be a problem. We'd figure it out. "Guess the stairs are going to be yellow." I climbed onto the banister and slid down the railing.

"I was right," Carly said. "You should have asked for help."

"It'll be fine. Yellow stairs are unique!"

She shrugged. "I suppose I can make it into an interesting mural."

"Sure!"

We walked to the diner, and I pulled the trading cart inside. A few people were sipping coffee at the counter, while others sat in the comfy, red leather booths. Mr. Carlson looked up from behind the counter and smiled. "My favorite customers. Come on in! What do you have for me today?"

"We'd like to trade for four lunches. We're working on New Hope's Finest again," I told him. "Plus, I have a critter I made special for Mrs. Carlson," I said in a low voice.

He grinned. "Betty, the kids are here with new critters."

Mrs. Carlson was all smiles again, and I tried to imagine what she'd looked like the day before, when she was sad. I'd never seen it.

I held out the cat for her. "Since you like the dog so much, I thought you'd like a kitty, too. Might make you smile on days when you feel like you can't."

She took it from me like it was a giant diamond. "This is exquisite. Just lovely. Thank you, Penny." She set her hand on my shoulder and squeezed. "Your creativity tickles me so, child. My Mary . . ." She sucked in a deep, wobbly breath. "My Mary was creative like you. It's wonderful."

"Thanks," I said quietly.

"Mr. Carlson will have to build a bigger shelf soon." She chuckled as she found a spot for the cat.

I held my breath, wondering if a hug was on its way. "I have others in the cart to trade for lunches. We're taking a break."

But no hug came. She frowned instead. "You kids are still working over there?"

"Yes, ma'am. You should come take a look."

"I will never, ever, go over there," she whispered, before darting back behind the counter.

I was so stunned, I didn't know what to say.

Old Mr. Smith, who spent most mornings at the diner, slid off his chair at the counter and came over. Took him a bit. He didn't move so fast. "What's this about you kids working at New Hope's Finest?"

I blinked a few times, still surprised by Mrs. Carlson's harsh words. I tucked my hands in my jean pockets. "We're cleaning it up so we can find a new buyer."

He pulled a toothpick out of his shirt pocket and stuck it between his back teeth. "Why now? It's been sitting idle for years."

All the chatter in the diner seemed to have stopped. A roomful of ears was fixed on us.

"Leave it be," Mr. Smith said. "That place ruined so many lives."

I cleared my throat. "I suppose that's why we're doing it. It's been making the whole town feel sorry for so long. It's time to change that." People wouldn't understand why I had to get New Hope back on the map, so I left that bit out.

Mr. Tyler from the gas station got up now, too, and

stood next to Mr. Smith. "And how are you kids going to do that?" He took off his ball cap and scratched his wild, curly hair. The dark strands seemed to be fighting with the gray ones over which got to be in control.

"There's four of us. We can do it." I held up a finger. "Although we could use a ladder. Do you have one, Mr. Smith?"

"Got one at home, but I'm not going near the Finest. You kids shouldn't be either."

I crossed my arms. "You can pick something from my trading cart in exchange."

"I don't want to be involved." Mr. Smith shook his head and went back to his seat.

Well, I certainly wasn't going to beg him to help. I'd have to do it myself.

"You kids shouldn't be up there," Mr. Tyler said.

I crossed my arms. "The mayor said we could, and she's in charge. So we're going to keep working."

I sat down, quickly ate lunch, and got back to the Finest to hang that wind chime. Maybe when people saw some progress, they'd change their mind and be more excited about the project. I had to work harder and faster. I had to hang that wind chime right away to stir up some excitement.

Carly, Chase, and Parker came up the driveway and started working on their projects again. "Be right back!" I told them, and I dashed across the street to the hardware store. "Mr. Gaiser, do you have a ladder I could rent?"

He walked out from the store's back room. "I do. But what do you need it for?"

"A project I'm doing at the Finest."

He crossed his arms and shook his head. "I don't want to be responsible if something goes wrong. What if you fell off the ladder? Find something else to do this summer."

I gritted my teeth, but I left the store and marched over to the site. I could do this myself.

I stacked up the records looped together in my wind chime, stuffed the whole thing into Carly's backpack, and zipped it up. The bicycle wheel hung out of the back of it.

I piled tires underneath a big maple tree to help me reach the first branch. It was at least ten feet off the ground. I stacked up seven tires, and then three next to that to help me get up on the taller pile. I put on the backpack and climbed up onto the tires. The bike tire bounced against my back. It was heavy.

Carly, Chase, and Parker stopped working and came over to watch me climb the tree.

"Are you sure you can do that?" Carly asked.

"I have to. I don't have a ladder. I'll be fine." The first branch was still just out of reach, but there was a big knot sticking out of the tree, so I stepped up onto that and grabbed the branch. I hung on, getting my balance. It was tough climbing with the backpack and the wheel weighing me down. Harder than I thought, but I wouldn't admit that.

I pulled myself up to the first branch and waited a bit, catching my breath. Then I moved up to another branch, and another. I peeked down at the ground and felt a little dizzy, I was so high up.

"That's far enough!" Carly hollered.

"I know," I responded. "Just let me hang this and I'll be right down." I wanted the chime to sway in the breeze, so I'd have to hang it far from the trunk. I'd have to crawl out along the branch to do that, which might sound easy, but seemed impossible from where I was sitting.

I lay on my stomach and wrapped my arms and legs around the tree, inching my way out to the edge of the limb. It was a thick branch, but it sagged a bit under my weight. *This was probably a bad, bad idea.*

"Penny, come back down. It's not worth it," Carly shouted.

"I've got this, don't worry." I had to find my courage to sit up and unload the backpack. It was so much higher than I'd imagined. So much shakier. My heart pounded. One wrong move and I would fall. And if I did, I'd probably die, or break every bone in my body. Is this what the doom painting had been warning me about? Should I turn back? I looked behind me, but climbing back down with the heavy backpack seemed scary, too. No, I couldn't give up now. I had to hang this wind chime so all those crabby customers at the diner could see what I was talking about. That there was possibility for this old, forgotten place.

I slowly sat up on the limb and stayed still for a few moments, making sure I had my balance. Leaves on tiny branches around me shook in the breeze, like they were worrying about me. "I'm okay," I hollered, even though I was nervous as all get out.

"Penny, please come down!" Parker shouted.

"Almost done." I slid one arm out of the backpack, then the other. I sat it on my lap with the wheel on top. The limb wobbled with every movement. I looped one leg around a small branch sticking out from the one I was on. While gripping the tree with one hand, I unzipped the backpack and lifted out the wind chime. The backpack fell to the ground and Carly screamed.

"I'm okay!" I reassured her. With one hand, I grabbed the big hook and hung it on the branch. It fit perfectly. "Almost done!"

I released the wheel and then the stack of records attached to the fishing line, letting it drop from the tree so the wind chime could swing in the breeze. The records plunked down in place, and I let out the breath I'd been holding. But that's when something jerked my leg, almost pulling me off the branch. I shook my foot. I realized one of the strings had wrapped around my ankle several times as it dropped, tugging on my leg. I grabbed the branch with both hands and lay on my belly, frightened I might fall.

"Penny!" Parker shouted.

I shook my leg, trying to free myself, but it was no use. I tried reaching my ankle, but my arm wouldn't stretch that far. There was no way for me to untangle the wire without toppling off the branch.

"We're going to get help!" Carly called.

"Okay!" I shut my eyes and tried to breathe slowly and deeply to stay calm. But my heart was a jackhammer. I was so far out on the branch, I was sure it would snap under me. I shimmied back toward the trunk as much as I could, but that wire wrapped around my ankle kept me from going too far. "I'm fine!" I shouted, more to calm myself down than anyone else.

That horrible doom painting must've made this happen. It had been a curse after all. Was there anyone on my family tree who could help me out of this tree?

I thought about Annie Edson Taylor, the first person to survive a trip over Niagara Falls in a barrel in 1901. She was on my family tree. *I'm the descendant of an incredible daredevil,* I reminded myself. But picturing her tumbling over a great big waterfall did not help me feel brave at that moment.

There was no one on my family tree to help me. Was there anyone in town who could? Or maybe no one would bother, since they'd all warned me to stay away. This was all my fault. Maybe they'd try to shut down the project for good.

CHAPTER 10

Seemed like hours had passed by the time Mr. Gaiser showed up with a ladder, but it was probably only ten minutes. Guess time creeps by when you're holding on for your life.

"My ladder's not tall enough to reach you," Mr. Gaiser said as he stood beneath the tree. "How did you get up there?"

I explained how I did it. "I'll give you ten things from my trading cart if you get me down. No—twenty."

"I'm too heavy to come up and get you. The branch would break," he said. "I'm calling the fire department."

"Okay." I tried not to sound scared, but I wasn't sure there was anyone who could get me down. My hands were getting numb from holding the tree so tight. Jagged bits of bark dug into my skin. The tree groaned and cracked, like it was deciding where to snap off the branch. I swear the wind was picking up, too, like it was going to help the tree toss me to the ground. *How many people die from falling out of trees every year?* I wondered.

The fire department showed up a few minutes later, along with a line of people from town. But there were so many other trees, they couldn't get their truck near me.

"We're working on a plan," one of the firefighters yelled. "You're doing great. Keep calm."

"Maybe you could pile up more tires and climb up to me," I shouted down to the crowd. My mouth was dry, and my throat was getting hoarse from hollering.

"The stack would be too unstable," Mr. Smith said.

Soon even more people from town were gathered under the tree. "Hang tight," Mr. Carlson said. "We'll figure something out. Mrs. Carlson is beside herself with worry right now."

Oh, I hated worrying her. But I noticed she wasn't there. She wasn't kidding when she said she'd never come to the Finest.

"Just hold on. You're doing great," Mr. Gaiser shouted.

"Thanks," I hollered back. But I did not feel like I was doing great. I remembered the poster from Mr. Hanes's room with the cat in the tree: "Hang in There, Baby!" What else could I do? I rested my head on the branch and wondered how scary it would be up here in the dark—if I didn't fall before then. What if I never got down? Maybe people would come from miles around to see the girl who lives in a tree. That might get us back on the map.

"I'm coming up to get you," Parker yelled, trying to scramble up the tire pile. But he slipped and tumbled to the ground.

Mr. Gaiser helped him to his feet and patted his head. "All right," he said, with a sigh. "I didn't want it to come to this, but there's one person who might be able to help. I'll be right back."

After he left, more and more people from town showed up. Some shouted words of encouragement. Others were wandering around the site, checking things out. A few went inside the building.

"This darn wind chime better look good," I grumbled to myself. *What's the world record for sitting in a tree?* I wondered. *Maybe I can break it. The record, not the tree limb!* Oh, it was scary if I stopped to think about it. So I closed my eyes and whistled and hummed to myself while I made plans for other creations from all the scraps below.

About half an hour after Mr. Gaiser left, I heard a rumble in the driveway. I opened my eyes and saw a rusty, white construction truck headed my way. It looked familiar.

"No way," I whispered to myself. "Is that Joe?"

The people gathered below me cleared a space for Joe to drive toward the tree. He could get closer than the fire truck had, since his truck was smaller.

Joe parked the truck and climbed out of the driver's seat. He put his hands on his hips and looked up at me. "You okay?" His voice sounded shaky, and I wondered if he was worried about me, or worried about being in town with all those folks gawking at him.

"I'm hanging in there." My arms were shaking from holding on so tight.

He blew out a breath. "I'll be right up to get you." He got back in the truck, and a big metal contraption slowly unfolded from the back of the truck. Then he climbed into the back compartment and strapped himself in with a harness.

Joe fiddled around with something inside the bucket, and it rose into the air. Soon Joe was right beside me. Shaking his head, he sighed. "I warned you about this place. What were you thinking?"

"I was thinking this record wind chime would look real nice hanging from this big tree. And it will, once you get me untangled."

He reached over and unwound the fishing line from

my leg. The string of records dropped from the tree and spun below us.

Joe held out his hand. "Let's get you down."

I swung my legs into the metal container and jumped in. The crowd below cheered, and I let out the longest breath ever. My legs shook, and I sat on the floor of the tiny box.

Joe moved a few levers, and the bucket lowered to the ground slowly. He hopped out, then helped me follow. My arms felt numb from holding on to that branch so tightly, for so long.

Parker ran over and hugged me. "I thought you'd be in that tree forever."

I hugged him back. "Nah, I knew I'd get down," I said. Even though that wasn't a hundred percent true.

We were surrounded by a crowd of people.

"You can take however many things you want from my trading cart," I said to Joe. "Empty it, if you want."

"No need," said Joe. "I'm just glad I could help get you down."

"But I need to pay you back somehow."

"No, you don't. Thankfully I got my truck to start, so I could get down here," Joe said.

I stepped back and looked up at the wind chime. The

records spun in the breeze. It looked even better than I'd imagined. "It's amazing! Let's make another one."

"I think one is enough." Mr. Gaiser chuckled from where he was standing in the crowd. "Now I'd better go unlock the shop. Not that there's going to be a line of people waiting for me." He shuffled off down the driveway.

Joe walked toward the building, and I followed him onto the porch. "Thanks, Joe. Guess that's the bad thing that happened cause of your doom painting. So it should be nice and easy from here on out," I said. "If you wanted to come back again or something."

"That's not a good idea. I'm just going to look around the place, and then I'll be on my way." He stepped inside the building.

Mr. Smith came over to me. "I wouldn't mind tinkering with those bikes, if you don't have a plan for them. Think I can get them working again."

"That'd be great!" I said.

"Used to fix up bikes when I was a kid." He scratched his head. "Guess I can understand why they all ended up back here, after what happened to poor Mary. But I can't bear to see them all rusty and broken."

I froze. "What do you mean about what happened to Mary? Mary Carlson?"

He nodded, and his eyes darted over to Mr. Carlson, who was standing on the other side of the yard, looking up at the trees. "She was riding her bike and got hit by a car coming out of the orphanage. This was right after it closed."

I felt like the breath was sucked out of me, and a swirl of sadness settled inside my lungs. I never knew how Mary died. Never had the heart to ask the Carlsons. "That's terrible." No wonder Mrs. Carlson hated this place.

"I think the bikes were the first things that got dumped back here." Mr. Smith rubbed the back of his neck. "Seems like some of the sorrow might be lifted if they weren't lying around."

"I think so, too. Thanks, Mr. Smith. I'll pay you back, somehow."

"No need. You're doing me a favor, letting me do this." He looped his hands together and stretched them out. "Makes me feel young again to have a big project ahead of me. Something I enjoyed as a kid."

I noticed other people picking through the stuff in the yard. I headed over to Chase and Parker as they sorted through more boxes. "We've got mounds of plastic soda bottles," Chase said. "Should we just leave them out for the trash?"

"Keep them." Those bottles would become something new. I could feel it, the same way I could feel my toes scrunching up against my old sneakers.

I noticed Joe heading for his truck and felt disappointed. I was hoping he'd stay a while, take a look around. I hurried over to him. "Thanks again for coming to get me. You don't have to leave so soon. There are a lot of neat things we could do around here with that truck."

He hung his head. "No one in town wants to see me near this place."

"But you're here now," I pointed out.

"It was an emergency. I won't be welcome again. Everyone blames me for the Finest falling through all those years ago."

"That's nonsense. It's not your fault."

"I left the doom painting here, didn't I?" Joe raised an eyebrow. "A person's creations hold power. Everything you make carries a little bit of you with it. Takes some of your intention."

A tingly feeling shot through me. "Never thought of it that way." I pictured the things I'd made. Was a little bit of me in them? All those tin can critters?

"Some say this land's been cursed ever since they closed the orphanage and forced the kids out," Joe said.

I never knew why it closed, just that it did. "Why did they close it, anyway?" I asked.

"Budget cuts." He closed his eyes. "All those kids. All those special kids, forced into homes, or sent off to live with relatives who didn't want them. Who didn't understand them."

My heart felt like someone was squeezing it with two hands. "How were they special?"

Joe looked up at the sky. "They had gifts. Special things they could do."

My insides went cold. "Like what?"

"Some had dreams that came true. Some claimed they could see the future. I remember one girl said she could talk to animals. Stuff most people couldn't do. Most of 'em were real creative. Incredible artists."

It took a few moments before I could say anything. "Could any of them see people . . . in shades of colors?" Maybe if I'd lived here ten years ago, *I* would have been sent here.

He shrugged. "Wasn't sure what each kid could do. Some didn't like to talk about it." He rubbed the side of his head, like maybe all these memories coming out hurt. "It wasn't a big home. Not more than forty kids. One floor for the boys, one for the girls."

"Why did they all end up here?"

Joe looked down, fumbling with something in his pocket. "Folks are scared of that kind of thing. They thought the kids were crazy, so they shipped them off. Gave up their own children, or backed out of adoptions. So this place was set up for the 'challenging' cases, as they called us."

"Us?" My voice cracked.

He settled his watery blue eyes on me. "Yes. I lived here when I was a child."

CHAPTER 11

As soon as he said it, Joe hurried to his truck, like he could run away from his words.

I chased him, my sneakers crunching against the stones and my mind stirring up a million questions. "Wait! Tell me about the other kids! What was your talent?"

He hopped into the seat of his truck, shaking his head. "Don't want to talk about it." He slammed the door.

I caught up to him and gripped the edge of his open window. "Fine. But will you come back and help here? You can have anything from my trading cart in exchange for using your truck."

A hurt look split his face. "Feels strange being back here, after everything that's happened. It's best for everyone if I keep to myself at home." He held up a hand. "Please, I have to go."

I stepped away and he backed out of the driveway, sending up a plume of dust. I stood in the middle of it, my mind feeling just as cloudy.

Mr. Carlson walked over and set his hand on my arm. "Some scary moments back there, Penny. I'm sure glad you're okay." He blew out a breath. "Do you think you could head over to the diner and talk to Mrs. Carlson? She's worried sick about you. Pains me so when she's upset."

"I'll go right away." I hated knowing that I'd upset her, especially now that I knew the terrible thing that had happened right in front of here.

I ran down the driveway, skidding on the stones, and dashed across the street to the diner. I burst through the front door, and Mrs. Carlson was sitting on a stool in front of the counter, gazing off.

The place was empty.

She noticed me, then pressed a hand over her mouth and ran to me. "You're okay!" She wrapped her arms around me in a hug, and I didn't wiggle away. Finally she stepped back. "What were you thinking, climbing that tree?"

I shrugged. "I didn't realize how high it was. But I was fine until the wind chime got wrapped around my ankle."

"You should have asked for help."

I just shrugged. "I don't need help."

Her wide eyes softened. "Everyone needs to ask for help, now and again."

I was not going to be sassy and tell her she was wrong. But my mama had told me otherwise.

She sighed. "But, Penny. I told you that place was cursed."

"I know that's what you said, but I don't think it is. Not anymore. I'm okay, aren't I? And we're going to turn the building into something wonderful." I paused. "I know a lot of bad things happened over there. I'm sorry about your daughter."

She sucked in a breath, but she nodded.

I softened my voice. "But the Finest will stay a sad, sad thing until we make it something good again."

She wrapped her arms around herself like she was cold. "It would be nice to believe that. But we heard words an awful lot like that from the businessmen when they convinced us to try the first time."

"But I'm not asking anyone for money. I'm not even asking anyone for help. I can do this on my own. I just want people to give me a chance."

She didn't say anything for a long while. So long, I started wondering if I should leave. Then she walked over to the window and stared down the street toward the Finest. She placed her hand on the window, like she was reaching out to touch the past. "It was going to be the loveliest salon."

"A beauty shop?" I asked.

She chuckled. "A salon is a place to discuss ideas. Art." She closed her eyes. "It was going to have the most beautiful gardens, and a big drawing room inside for meetings and lectures. They'd serve tea and goodies. I came up with a few delectable scone recipes while the investors were working. I thought I might be able to sell them to the owners to put on their menu." She sighed, and the sound was so sad it took some of the breath out of my lungs, too. "After Mary died, I poured my heart into making plans for that place, thinking it could distract me from the pain."

Mrs. Carlson's color was fading. I hated seeing her like that. "Maybe it could still be that wonderful thing. There's lots of room over there. A great big yard."

Mrs. Carlson let out a long sigh. "I just don't know if I could ever put my faith in that place again. Or if I could spend time so close to the place where . . . it happened."

I wanted to tell her that working over at the Finest would make her happy. That everyone's color had started glowing stronger once they got to work over there. But that's not something you can really explain, now is it?

Before bed, I sat down next to Grauntie on the couch, trying to figure out how to ask her all my questions. I wanted to know more about the kids from the orphanage. If she was having a good night, she might remember something.

She narrowed her eyes at me, leaning back like she was checking to be sure I was really there. We weren't one for sitting next to each other much. Grauntie liked her space, and so did I. Parker was curled up in a chair, reading a book.

"Something wrong?" Grauntie asked.

"Nope." I shrugged. "Just wondering if you ever met any of the kids who used to live at the orphanage."

She looked up at the ceiling, thinking. I wondered if that helped the memories spill out. "Can't say that I did," she said. "But Gert went to school with a few of them. One boy had a weird name, like a bird. Goose? Robin, maybe."

I froze. "Do you mean Wren? Wren, with the freckles?"

She snapped her fingers. "Yes, that's right. Wren. Told me he was speckled with freckles. Said he was brown like a little wren, too. Don't see kids like that around here too often. You know, besides you two."

Wren with the freckles had brown skin like mine? I looked at Parker, my eyes big and round, but he just looked confused.

Grauntie worked her lips back and forth like she was figuring what words should come out next. "Not sure if your mother ever met any of them, that summer she was here."

My eyes popped wide open. I'm surprised I didn't fall right off the couch. "Mama was here?"

Parker closed his book and came over to sit next to us.

Grauntie nodded. "Came to stay with me right after she graduated high school. Thought the name of the town was a good sign for her future."

"My mama, Darlene Parker, with hair like mine?"

"Yes, she's my older sister's granddaughter." Frowning, she patted her lap and looked down at her feet. "Where's my pocketbook? I need my pocketbook."

"Right next to you on the couch," I said.

She turned and grabbed it. "Of course. There it is."

"No one ever told me Mama lived with you, Grauntie." This was a huge piece of information. How could I not know this? Why had Mama never mentioned it? Or anyone else, for that matter? "You're sure?"

Grauntie rubbed her hands up and down her thighs. "Of course I am. Said she was going to find a job here, but never did get work. I don't know how she spent her time. She never was home. And she wasn't here long. Just up and left one day. No goodbye, no thank-you note."

"Where did she go?" I asked.

Grauntie turned up a hand. "Don't know."

"Mama was here. Right here in New Hope. Right in this *house*." As far as I knew, while Grauntie didn't remember everything, she didn't make stuff up. And maybe this had happened long enough ago that it was still stuck in her mind like a movie clip. "Are you really, really sure?"

"Am I sure your mother lived with me for two months? Of course I am. Ate all my cookies. Loved my cat." She stood up and scanned the room. "Where is that darn cat?"

I looked at Parker. His eyes were wide.

"It's been a long day, children. We should get to bed," Grauntie said.

I kept doing the math: Mama graduated high school when she was eighteen. She had us the next year in April, when she was nineteen. I knew it took nine months for a baby to come.

It all added up. Did Mama meet our Daddy right here in New Hope? A boy with brown skin and freckles?

 ̶o̶t̶t̶t̶

Before bed, I locked myself in the bathroom. I brushed my teeth, then sat in front of the big, long mirror on the back of the door. I stared in it, looking for a clue as to who I might be. My eyes were green, like Mama's. No mystery there. Same hair color as Mama's, too, but hers hadn't been quite so wild. My puff of hair didn't look like Mrs. Carlson's tight curls, either. No, people liked to ask me if I'd been electrocuted, that's how wild it was, so I couldn't say I was part black for sure. Nothing in my face answered my questions about who I was.

Once, before Mama died, an old lady at the grocery store had crinkled up her nose and called us mutts. I laughed and barked 'cause I thought it was funny, but Mama slapped my face—the one and only time she ever did that. I didn't remember much about Mama, but I sure remembered that moment.

"That's not funny," Mama had hissed at me, with tears in her eyes. I was so shocked by her hitting me, I didn't even ask why it wasn't funny. Parker and I pretended we were puppies all the time—kitties, too. But when I was a little older, I heard someone else call us mixed, and I figured out what that old lady had meant. Mutts were a mix of different dogs. And Parker and me weren't one thing, either: not just white, not just black, or Hispanic, or Indian, or whatever my daddy was.

Never saw many other people who were mixed like me. So it seemed like a special thing, not bad. Mama even said so once. "Why is mixed bad?" I had asked her one day, after seeing someone pointing at us at McDonald's.

She cupped her hand under my chin and looked me right in the eye. "Mixed isn't bad. It's magnificent. There is no one quite like you. Be proud of that."

And I was. But that didn't mean I didn't have questions.

I pressed my nose against the mirror and stared until my eyes crossed. Who was I? Now that I knew about Mama's visit, and Wren with the freckles, I might be able to get some answers.

First thing the next morning, Parker and I walked to Joe's. I had to find out if Wren had known a girl with red hair like mine. I rang the bell and rapped on the door, but there was no answer. Was he going to hide inside for the rest of his life? Made me so sad the way people treated him, the way he thought he was no good.

"I think he wants to be left alone," Parker said.

"We're not going to give up on him. We'll try again later. Let's go to the Finest," I said.

When we got there, Mr. Smith was back, working on the bikes, humming a tune. His color was growing brighter. Mr. Tyler was collecting old gas cans and other bits of metal. A few other people from town poked through junk piles nearby or wandered around the site. I was surprised folks had come back. Thought they'd just dashed over the day before to sneak a peek of me in the tree so they could gab about it later.

Parker ran over to Chase, and I joined Carly, who was sorting bottles into piles of the same color. "What are we going to do with these?" she asked. "There are so many."

There were hundreds. How could we find a use for

all of them? Then I remembered the story of George Washington Carver from my *Notable People* book. He found three hundred different uses for peanuts. Peanuts! Certainly I could find a few uses for plastic bottles. I wondered if there were any inventors on my family tree. My daddy? Or maybe George Washington Carver himself was on my tree. It was possible. He was going on the list when I got home. *I am the descendant of a brilliant inventor.*

"Three hundred ways to use peanuts," I whispered to myself. "Okay, George Washington Carver, I can do it with bottles." I picked up a bottle, but instead of an empty plastic container, this time I saw possibilities. If I cut off the top, the bottom could be used to grow flowers, like in a pot, or we could paint it like a vase for cut flowers. My mind was swirling with ideas, like a merry-go-round on hyperdrive.

Then I noticed all the different colored caps still on the bottles, like splotches of paint. "Take all the caps off and put them in a pile," I told Carly. "Sort them by color." I picked up a clear, empty soda bottle and turned it around in my hands. "Do we have scissors?"

Carly nodded. "I saw some in an old toolbox by the metal scraps."

I found the scissors, then settled in among the mountain of bottles. I used scissors to poke a hole above the black base of one bottle, then cut shapes out of the sides. I held it up for Carly.

She tilted her head and smiled. "That looks like a flower."

I cut out a few more while Carly twisted a cap off a bottle and tossed it into a pile. "I think we have more colors of caps than we do paint," she said.

My fingers tingled. "What to do with those caps . . ." I snapped my fingers. "We could make a collage out of them."

"Yeah!" Carly said. "On the fence."

"That will look amazing!" I said. "I'm so glad you decided to work here. You really have a lot of great ideas."

Her cheeks flushed. "No one's ever said that to me before. That I'm great at anything, I mean."

"Well, you are."

"Thanks," Carly said. "I wish I could get Mama to come work down here. I think she'd like it. Better than just sitting home."

"Bring her along!" Just then, I heard a chugging noise coming up the driveway. My head snapped up. I'd heard that sound before! Sure enough, a big white truck was making its way onto the site.

"Joe came!" I sprinted over to him. I waved as he drove up the hill, and he waved back. I was excited to think he might be here to work. But even more important, I had to learn more about Wren.

He pulled up next to me and rolled down the window. "Being back in town yesterday was nice. Didn't realize how much I'd missed it. But I need to find a way to convince people to trust me again."

"And?" I asked.

"An idea exploded in my brain." He made a fist and snapped it open. "If I get rid of my painting supplies, I can't do any more paintings. So they're packed up in my truck."

"Genius!"

Joe was smiling widely. "Could you use my supplies here?"

"You bet. Let's put it all inside."

Joe parked the truck and started unloading his things, so I grabbed a few boxes too. "Can you tell me more about Wren with the freckles?" I asked as we hauled his stuff inside.

His color faded so quickly, I thought he was going to disappear. "Not much to say. Knew him from the orphanage."

"Was he here the summer of 1971?"

He closed his eyes and nodded quickly. "Yeah, we were both graduating high school."

I tried to keep my voice calm. "Did he know a girl with red hair, same color as mine?"

But before Joe could respond, Mr. Tyler marched over and pointed his finger at him. "What are you doing here? Yesterday was just an exception, so you could get this girl out of the tree."

Joe said nothing.

Mr. Tyler crossed his arms. "We don't want you here. My shed burned down after you left that doom painting. I lost everything inside it."

Joe looked down and nodded.

Mr. Tyler's words hurt my heart, and he wasn't even talking about me. An anger swelled up inside me. I stood tall and proud like my ancestors, and put my hands on my hips. "He's not causing any trouble. He's trying to stop trouble. He's donating his art supplies so he can't make any more doom paintings."

Mr. Tyler's eyes darkened. "I can't work on this if he's here."

I needed Joe here so he could tell me more about Wren. But I also didn't like seeing him treated so badly. He didn't create the doom paintings on purpose. None of what happened at the Finest was his fault—so why didn't he have a right to work here if he wanted to? My heart pounded and I tipped up my chin. "Then I guess you'll have to leave. Because Joe is staying."

Mr. Tyler glared at me, then stomped off back to town, his color disappearing as he left.

People were staring at me. I swallowed hard, but I wasn't going to let anyone who was going to be mean to Joe work here. No one on my family tree would stand for behavior like that. I imagined them all nodding in agreement as I put my hands on my hips and raised my voice. "If anyone else has a problem with Joe working here, you might as well leave now."

Two people sorting through one of the piles dropped what they were holding and left. Another stepped off the porch and walked down the driveway, not looking our way. But with reluctant shrugs, the others stayed, and got back to what they were doing.

"People will never forgive me," Joe said, holding two cans of paint.

"They will, once we have this place all fixed up.

Especially if you help." I grabbed another box. "Do you know what this place was even supposed to be? I keep hearing lots of different ideas."

He headed inside and set down the cans. "I think the developers told people whatever they wanted to hear. Everybody had different ideas about what the most amazing tourist attraction would be."

"So they never said for sure exactly what they were building?" No wonder I'd been hearing so many different ideas.

"Just that it would be the finest thing in all of North Carolina. I was supposed to use my truck to paint in the final word on that sign. But they never would tell me what the word was going to be," Joe said as we walked into the building.

"I wonder if we'll ever know." I looked around the big front room. "Even though this place caused so much disappointment, I get an exciting feeling here. Was it always like that?"

"It was a special place," he said.

"You said all the kids who stayed here could do special things. What was Wren's talent?" I bit my bottom lip, wondering if I was asking too many questions.

It took a moment, but Joe's smile returned. "He was a neat kid. He could paint a picture that looked so real, you'd swear it was a photograph. Never seen anything like it."

"Wow."

"Suppose that's why we got along so well. I could paint pictures of people and places I'd never seen. Freaked some people out, but not Wren. He loved to watch me work. Since we both loved painting, we thought we'd start a business together someday."

"Why didn't you?" I asked, setting the box inside the building.

He walked outside onto the front porch and sighed.

I followed him.

"Wren and I got in a big fight, and we never talked again."

"Never?" That seemed unbelievable. "What was the fight about?"

He shook his head and looked away. "Don't want to talk about it."

"Do you know where he is now? Is he an artist living in a big city?" *My maybe-dad could be famous*, I thought.

He crossed his arms and sighed. "I'm already uncomfortable working here. And I'm not going to be able to stay if you keep asking questions about Wren. It's just too hard with the way things ended between us."

"Okay." I shut up 'cause I didn't want him to leave. But there was so much I needed to know! How else could I learn more about Wren? "Did anyone else in town know him? Maybe I could ask around."

He stared at me with cold eyes. "Do not ask people about Wren. Please, just leave the past in the past."

I blinked a few times, not sure what he meant, or what to say.

"I'm going to sort all my stuff," he told me, heading back inside.

I sighed, realizing I hadn't gotten an answer to my most important question: Did Wren know a girl with red hair like mine?

Parker was across the yard, sitting against the fence, sorting through bolts and screws, and I plopped down next to him. But my mind was still turning over Joe's warning words: *Don't ask about Wren.* Why?

"Mr. Gaiser doesn't know it, but he's missing his keys again. He left them on the windowsill in the big front room of the Finest," Parker said.

"I'll let him know."

And that's when it hit me—the perfect idea. I didn't have to ask around about Wren. I should try to find him. And I knew how. At least, I thought I knew who could.

I took a deep breath. I'd never asked Parker to find me anything before, and this was a big thing to ask for. But I figured Mama's rule about not asking for help didn't apply to Parker since he was my brother. And especially since I was in charge and this is what we needed to do. "Can you find missing people?"

He scratched his nose. "Never have before."

"You need to find Wren."

"I don't *try* to find missing things, Penny. I just know about them when the time is right." He tossed a bolt into a pile.

"Well, you've got to at least try. I think there's a real good chance Wren is our dad," I said. "Maybe he'd want to take us in."

He wouldn't look at me. "Don't want to."

I practically toppled over in surprise. "What? You don't want to know who our dad is?"

"If he wanted us, he'd be around. We're not supposed to beg; Mama said so in her letter." He dropped a handful of bolts onto the ground. "Sure wish she left *me* a letter so I could boss you around."

I groaned. "I don't boss. I just know what to do. Besides, Mama told me everything we need to know. She was probably too weak to write another whole letter."

Parker bit his lip and nodded. "I suppose."

"We don't know why our dad wasn't around. If we find him, we can ask him. That's why I need you to try."

He said nothing.

Oh, this was frustrating. "We're not going to ask him to take us in. But maybe he would just want to."

"I don't want to find him."

"Parker! I'm in charge and I'm telling you to try and find him."

He stood and glared at me. "No." He walked away.

No? Parker always listened to me. I couldn't believe it! I got up to chase after him, but before I could, I saw Miss Meriwether coming my way, wearing her business suit and high heels.

She did *not* look like she was ready to pick up a paintbrush and start working. Her eyes were wide, and her cheeks were red. Her voice trembled. "What in the world are you doing here?"

CHAPTER 12

I brushed off my hands and made myself smile. "Hello, Mayor. Sure is coming along, isn't it?"

She quickly blinked her eyes a few times. "I thought you were joking around when you said you were going to fix up the Finest. You're just a kid."

"True, but I'm not one to joke, ma'am. And you said I could."

"I was being sarcastic," she said.

"Well, I didn't know that. But we got started, and it looks great so far."

She pinched the bridge of her nose. "This isn't a good idea."

I crossed my arms, frustrated at yet another person telling me this was a bad idea. "Why?"

She put her hands on her hips and looked around. "We had our hopes destroyed before. I don't know what will happen to this town if our dreams are crushed again."

She closed her eyes. "It's my job to protect the people here, and I let them down. I should've known the investors were scam artists."

My heart pounded. Miss Meriwether couldn't stop our work on the Finest now. She couldn't. How would we get back on the map? Whether that was going to bring Wren home or bring some new family to town that wanted us, I didn't know. I just knew the Finest had to reopen. And it was important for other people, too. All these people who were finding their glow again. I couldn't let her stop us.

She stared at me, and I stared back at her. I tried to imagine all the amazing people on my family tree standing beside me, cheering me on. I closed my eyes and felt them around me. "But what can folks lose this time?" I opened my eyes and looked at her. "They're not giving money. Just their time, because they want to. What if this works out? What if we turn it into something new and sell it?"

"I'm sorry, but no." Miss Meriwether cupped her hands around her mouth and shouted, "Stop your work, everyone. Please stop your work."

People paused, and a few walked toward her. "What's going on?" Mr. Smith asked.

"Penny was mistaken when she thought I said she could work on the Finest," Miss Meriwether said.

Mr. Smith scratched his head. "I was skeptical at first too, but things are coming along nicely. Lots of people are just showing up and helping out without being asked."

"I'm not willing to see this town let down again." Miss Meriwether shook her head.

Mr. Gaiser said, "I'd really like to see this become something again. Please."

I felt the power of hope and determination from my family swelling behind me. What were the right words to fix this? "If you shut this down, we might never get all these people this excited about something again." I thought about peaceful protestor Mahatma Gandhi. Yep, he was the one I needed from my tree. I widened my stance and tipped up my chin. "I'm related to the great Mahatma Gandhi. He fought for India's independence from the British Empire. He led protests and marches. Sometimes he fasted—for weeks! I'd do it, Miss Meriwether. Do you want me to lead all these folks in protests? Do you want us to stop eating?" *I'm the descendant of an amazing leader.*

She sighed and opened her mouth. Then closed it. Then raised an eyebrow. "You're related to Gandhi?"

I paused. "He's on my family tree."

She pressed her lips together. "I just hate seeing people get their hopes dashed."

"Could people feel any worse than they do now?" I asked. "Opening this place could get us back on the map, and then who knows all the wonderful things that could happen."

Joe wandered over.

Miss Meriwether looked at him like he was a ghost. "Joe Clark?" she whispered.

"Yes, ma'am." He studied the ground. "Never thought I'd come anywhere near this place. But it feels good to be making it something special again. To make things right after so long. Please let us keep working."

She watched people scurrying around the site. "I haven't seen so many folks from town in the same spot in years. And they seem so . . . energized." She let out a long breath, and her shoulders slumped. "I guess since so many of you are interested in doing this, you may carry on. I'll make sure our code enforcers take a look at the building to be sure all the electrical and plumbing is working, and that we have the proper paperwork in place for a sale. I suppose it won't hurt to spruce it up. But I can't promise we're going to be able to sell this to anyone."

"Thanks!" I knew I'd change her mind—with a little help from my family tree.

"I'll be checking in each day," she said, before walking away down the driveway.

Joe clapped his hands together. "Wonderful. I was just coming up with plans for a tree house."

"Wow!" This project was growing like I'd never imagined.

"The kids at the orphanage always wanted one." Joe looked up at the trees with his hands on his hips, smiling. "Wren and I used to talk about building one . . ." He stopped abruptly. "I'm going to draw up some plans. I know just the tree I'm going to use, too."

He looked happier than I'd ever seen him. Seemed like a bad moment to pester him about Wren and ruin the mood, so I kept my lips sealed. But I still had some time for questions, now that Joe had a big project bringing him back here every day.

Mr. Carlson walked up the driveway and stopped, looking over the place, nodding. He saw me, smiled, and walked up to me. "This place is looking great."

"Hi! What are you doing here?" I wanted to tell him how sorry I was that Mary died right in front of this place, but I didn't want his smile to disappear 'cause of me bringing up such a sadness.

"Curiosity got the best of me." He walked toward a pile of big metal pieces and chuckled. "You could make some big tin can critters out of these things."

He was right—the pile of junk was filled with possibilities. I could see them taking shape in my mind. My head pounded with ideas for the old paint cans and rusted tools lying around. Things started to wiggle and wobble. "You could help me. We could have a giant sculpture exhibit out here."

"Sure." Mr. Carlson smiled and smacked his hands together. "This is going to be wonderful."

"We're going to make something amazing, I just know it." I lugged out a big silver trash can with a lid. A smaller trash can made a great head. I circled the pile, looking for something else that stood out. Two rakes caught my eye, the big wide kind you use for leaves. I grabbed them both. Their poles were broken, but I didn't need those. The metal part would make amazing wings. "I can make an angel!"

Mr. Carlson held up a tire rim. "Here's the halo."

I gathered a pile of other things I'd need to put it

together, then stood back to survey it. "I don't think glue is going to work on this."

Mr. Carlson rubbed his chin. "No, you'll need to weld these pieces together. Mr. Gaiser knows how to do that."

"I'll find him!" I went into the building. "Mr. Gaiser?"

"Upstairs!"

I jogged up the stairs and found him in one of the rooms. "Someone was smart enough to cover all these windows with wood," he said. "They're in perfect shape. I just need to get my ladder and pull the boards off outside."

"I'm sure Joe would let you use his bucket truck."

Mr. Gaiser grumbled under his breath, "That's not necessary."

I put my hands on my hips, sick of this nonsense. "Joe brought all his painting gear here, so he can't make doom paintings anymore."

A bushy eyebrow poked up over one of his eyes. "I think it's bad luck, him even being here. Not so sure I feel comfortable working with him around."

This was ridiculous. Mr. Tyler left the project because of Joe, and now I was going to lose Mr. Gaiser, too? I couldn't risk that. He knew how to do so many helpful things. So I thought about the folks on my family tree and realized I'd have to add a new branch for a real good peacemaker. But who?

I snapped my fingers. King Kamehameha. I remembered reading how he united all the warring clans of the Hawaiian Islands, became a king, and Hawaii was officially established. There was a legend that whoever could move the giant Naha Stone would become the islands' greatest king. Kamehameha flipped that rock over when he was fourteen. If someone on my family tree could do all that, then, lordy, I could certainly get a few angry folks to get along. *I am the descendant of a great king!*

I took on a serious tone. "Mr. Gaiser, Joe is here helping, just like everyone else. He doesn't want to hurt anyone, and he's not bad luck. But I won't stand for people being unkind to him. You're a good person, Mr. Gaiser. I know you won't be mean."

He frowned and scratched his head. "I suppose I'm not mean. I'll just steer clear of him."

It wasn't the best answer, but it would do. For now. "Thank you."

"I was skeptical of your work here at first, but I really hope bringing this building back to life will bring business to town," Mr. Gaiser mused. "I'd love to see some other projects spring up. No one's bought materials from my store to do any renovations or put up new homes or sheds in years. Imagine everyone 'round here finding hope again."

"It would be wonderful, wouldn't it? Now, I'm making a giant tin can critter, and I don't think the glue will hold it. Can you weld it? I've got plenty to trade for in my cart."

"Sure can. I'll bring the stuff tomorrow. My wife's coming then, too. She always thought this place was going to be a botanical garden. Told me she wants to plant some flowers."

That would certainly be a fine addition. "Great!" Things were going so well, we'd have this place open for a buyer in no time. Thank goodness the doom painting I found hadn't ruined things here. Glad I didn't have to worry about that anymore.

When I left the building, I caught a glimpse of Joe working by himself in the corner, cutting off big branches from the tree where he was going to build the house. Seemed like that tree was glowing, like it was promising good things to come. But I felt bad that Joe was alone, so I wandered over to say hi before I got to work on my super-sized critters.

"Can't believe I'm finally doing this," he said. "Building the tree house. I've wished for a long time that I could make things right here, and suddenly it seems like maybe I can. I don't know if I'll ever earn everybody's forgiveness, but if I could see this place thriving, I'd be a happy man again."

I wanted that for him, almost as much as I wanted a home. "Were you happy when you lived here at the orphanage?"

He leaned against the tree. "Yes. It was great. Our caretakers were kind and loving. Accepted us, despite our . . . talents. And the children all got along. Everyone in town was wonderful to us, donating old clothes and food. Leaving presents at Christmastime. That's why it was so sad when the orphanage closed. It was like the heart of the town stopped beating."

And it started back up for a while when people thought it was going to reopen, I thought. "If you lived here as a kid, how did you end up with the Clarks?"

He threw another big branch onto a pile. "I was seventeen when the orphanage closed. Most of the younger kids were adopted by families in other communities. The Clarks' oldest child had just moved out, so they adopted me. I was so surprised they went through the whole process, even though I was almost an adult. But they wanted me to always have a home."

My heart squeezed a bit. That's the kind of family I wanted. "Where are they now?"

"They were older when they adopted me. To be honest, I think they also needed help around the house, help with the business. I learned a trade, and it was nice to have a place to go." He looked down at the ground and his voice softened. "They both died within two years of adopting me, though. I've been in that big old house by myself ever since."

Made me sad. Joe had been orphaned twice. "Where did Wren go when the orphanage closed?"

He narrowed his eyes. "Thought you weren't going to ask about him."

"The conversation just kind of took us there." I crossed my fingers, hoping I could keep him talking.

He studied a stick he was holding. "He was seventeen, too. We were both just about to graduate. No one stepped forward to adopt him, so he stayed with me and the Clarks."

"Do you think he met a girl with red hair staying here for the summer?"

He opened and closed his mouth a few times before

speaking. "I don't know everything he was doing. And you're taking me back to a difficult time. Let's just leave the past where it is. Wren and I were great friends, and then we fought." He broke his stick in half.

I nodded. "Sorry things ended that way." I paused, hoping he'd say more, but he didn't. "Okay. I'll see you tomorrow."

I left him by the tree and spent some time searching for all the right parts for my giant tin can critters.

Around dinnertime, I found Parker so we could walk home together. He hadn't said a word to me since our fight about finding Wren.

We walked in silence until I said, "I'm sorry you're mad at me, but I'm just trying to keep us together. I have to look after you, and how can I do that if we get split up in foster homes?"

"Thought we were going to live in the wild if that happened, instead." He shrugged. "Might be fun."

Easy for him to say. He wouldn't have to do all the planning and worrying. "Maybe. But I still think finding our daddy is important. Even if it's just to learn a few things about him."

"Like what?" he asked.

"We know Mama was Irish and German. That's

where her people came from. But what about our dad? He could be anything." I felt like a puzzle with a few pieces forever missing. And who wants a puzzle like that? The picture would never be complete.

Parker stopped walking. "Penny, I'd rather not know where he is than know he doesn't want us. And maybe I'm old enough now that I don't need you taking care of me or telling me what to do. I want to be the boss of me."

I was so stunned I didn't know what to say.

He ran off toward the house without me, and I trudged along, wondering why I was working so hard to keep us together when he didn't seem to care one bit.

CHAPTER 13

When I finally got home, I hurried to the mailbox just like I'd been doing every day since I sent my letter. And this time, there was a letter addressed to me from the map company. I sat on the front porch steps and ripped it open.

> Dear Miss Porter,
>   Thank you for your interest in our maps. Our latest map will be released on July 1st and available in stores near you.
>   Sincerely,
>   David Charter, CEO Charter Maps

That was four weeks away. But he didn't even say a word about the Finest or adding New Hope. I unfolded a small sheet of paper folded up inside the note.

> *Dear Penny,*
> *Thanks for your letter. We only include*

cities and towns of a certain size on our maps and others with particular interest to our customers. Sounds like you've got a very exciting project going on. I'd love to see a picture when you're done! Good luck! I'll send you a complimentary copy of our map when it's released.

Sheila Blakeley,
Secretary to CEO David Charter

She probably wanted the picture to show to the president and prove we deserved to be on the map! I walked inside, waving the letter. "Parker, the new map comes out July first. We've got four more weeks to get back on the map." That's when I noticed Parker was sitting on the couch by himself. "Where's Grauntie?" I asked.

"Back in my bedroom," she hollered. "I need your help."

Parker and I shared a concerned look, then headed her way, even though we usually weren't allowed in her room.

The door was open so we stepped inside, my toes disappearing in her shaggy, pink rug. "What is it?"

Grauntie was emptying her big glass display cases. "Mr. Gaiser called and said you kids were fixing up New Hope's Finest." Her eyes were wide and full of color.

"Yes, so we can find a new buyer to finally open it," I explained.

"I want you to take my snow globe collection down there and put it on display." She stuffed a globe into a box and added the box to the pile of them on the floor next to her.

"Are you sure? You love those so much." Plus, what would I do with several hundred snow globes? I needed to get rid of stuff, not bring more down there!

"The world should be able to enjoy them. Who knows how long I'll be kicking around, anyway?"

"Don't say that." I felt a shock of fear. If Grauntie was gone, we'd be gone, too.

"No one in my family has lived longer than eighty, so I'm already pushing the envelope on my, my . . . longevity," she replied.

"All right. We can take them down there for you." I watched her work for a minute. Grauntie didn't seem as grumpy as usual, so I thought I'd take a chance. "Did anyone ever tell you who our daddy is?"

She sat on her bed with a Christmas snow globe on her lap. "No. Nobody knew. Your mama wouldn't say who he was. I didn't see her too often after that summer she stayed here. Her grandma, my sister, and I didn't always see eye to eye. Years would go by without us talking."

"Do you think it could be that boy you told us about, Wren?" My heart fluttered just thinking about it.

"The bird boy?" She shrugged. "Never saw her with anybody. She never mentioned anyone." Grauntie took a good long time to get back to her feet, then brushed her hands together. "That railing on the back steps is loose. We need someone to fix it."

"I'll make sure it gets done," I said.

Parker and I left the room, and I set both my hands on his shoulders, looking him in the eye. "I know you can find Wren if you try."

Parker stepped back. "I told you, stop bossing me around."

"Do I have to get Mama's letter out and read it to remind you who's in charge?" I asked. I hated being mean, but this was for our own good. For *both* of us.

"You can read the letter, but you can't make me look for him."

He was right. I couldn't make him. I'd have to try something different to convince Parker to help me. "All right. Then help me fix the railing on the back steps," I said.

"Shouldn't we ask Mr. Gaiser to do it for a trade?"

"I've been pestering him too much for help. And I had to beg him to keep working on the Finest, even though Joe is there. He might get mad if I ask him for one more thing."

"Then how are we going to fix it?"

"You're not going to like this, but we're going to use the glue. Just plug your nose while you're helping me."

I got the glue and had Parker hold the railing against the house while I squeezed out a big lump of it. When the rail was glued in place, I stood back and looked at it. "That should be fine," I said with a nod.

卌

Since Parker wouldn't help find Wren, the next morning he went to the Finest, and I headed to the diner. I didn't want to bother Joe with more questions and scare him off. But maybe the Carlsons would know about Wren.

The bells on the door jangled as I walked inside. I sat at the counter, and Mrs. Carlson came out from the kitchen, cradling a cup of coffee in her hands. "I'm surprised to see you here. It's not lunchtime yet. Why aren't you working at the site?" She took a sip of her drink.

I paused for a moment, not quite sure how to explain what I wanted to know. "Since I've been spending so much time at the Finest, I've just been wondering about all those kids who lived at the orphanage. Joe doesn't like to talk about it much. But I heard they were . . . special. Did you know any of them?"

She smiled. "Of course. The diner was a popular place for them to hang out. Especially the teenagers."

"Did you know any of the teenagers? Maybe someone named Wren?"

She paused, then shook her head. "That name doesn't sound familiar. Why do you ask?"

"Joe mentioned him, that's all. I'm curious what the kids around here were like." I took a deep breath. "I just found out my Mama stayed here one summer with my Grauntie. The summer the orphanage closed. I'm trying to figure out who might have known her. Did you ever meet her? She had hair the same color as mine, and her name was Darlene."

"Your mother lived here? I'm sorry to say I don't think I met her. Not that I remember, anyway." She studied her mug for a moment, turning it 'round and 'round on the counter. "That was quite a while ago. Must be hard, not having a mother."

I swallowed hard. "It's fine. We don't have a daddy, either. We're used to it by now. We get by." I suppose saying words like that would have hurt someone else's heart. But not the way mine was all boarded up. The truths just bounced right off it. I stood up to leave. "I should get back. It's too bad you can't come see how much work we've done."

"You be careful over there." One corner of her mouth curled up. "Stay out of those trees, now."

I laughed. "I will."

Disappointed that I hadn't learned anything new from Mrs. Carlson, I decided to stop by the mayor's office to ask Miss Meriwether about Wren, but she wasn't in. Mr. Gaiser said he didn't know him, either.

It was like Wren was a ghost.

CHAPTER 14

The library was across the street from the mayor's office, so I headed there to see if there were any articles about the orphanage closing. Maybe a newspaper story would mention some of the kids and I could learn something—anything—about Wren.

The librarian, Miss Mullins, looked up when I walked inside the cool, dark building. She set down her book. "Why, hello. How may I help you? Haven't had a visitor here in days."

"Maybe 'cause so many folks are working over at the Finest, fixing it all up."

She nodded. "I heard about that. It would be nice to see things work out, but they probably won't. That's how it goes around here, you know."

I sighed. "You might change your mind once you see it." I shoved my hands in my pockets. "Since I've been working over there, I was hoping to find some information about the orphanage closing down."

She stood and smoothed her skirt. "I'm sure we still have some articles from the old *New Hope Weekly Crier*."

"New Hope had a newspaper?" I asked.

"A weekly edition. Stopped printing quite a few years back. Any copies would be on microfiche. I'll get you set up." Miss Mullins went into a back room and returned with a box of film reels. She searched through the box and picked one out. "This has copies of the paper from the spring and summer of 1971. That's when the orphanage closed."

I followed her to a small room with a big viewer on a table. She put the film on a spool and flipped on a switch. The pages of the newspaper were magnified, glowing on the screen. "Turn this crank on the right to flip through the pages."

"Thanks!" I settled in a chair and she left the room. I turned the crank, flipping through the past. The *Weekly Crier* was filled with ads for businesses around town. Mr. Gaiser had hammers on sale the week of April 11th. The Carlsons' diner had a roast beef platter special.

Then I found an article titled ORPHANAGE CLOSING AFTER FIFTY YEARS. There was a picture of the building with a few kids standing in front of it. But I didn't see anyone with freckles like mine. "'It's a sad day,' said orphanage director Tom Perkins," I read in the article. "'We're not the only orphanage falling victim to budget cuts. But I doubt any town will miss their children as much as we'll miss ours.'"

It was almost like I could feel the sadness that must've washed across the town.

I read over a few more articles, all of them reciting the facts I already knew, but I saw no mention of Wren, and no quotes from him, either. Dang.

I scrolled through more pages and found an article titled NEW HOPE FOR THE CLOSED ORPHANAGE? It talked about plans to turn the building into a grand attraction. I read the article twice, and I could see why people had gotten so excited. The Donovan brothers, the developers chosen to take on the project, promised it would bring visitors from far and wide and change the town forever. But I didn't learn anything new, and there was nothing about Wren or Joe being involved.

I skipped past a few more ads, then I froze. LOCAL GIRL STRUCK AND KILLED, I read. There was a big picture of a beautiful little girl with puffy pigtails tied up in thick yarn bows. "Mary Carlson, Age 11," read the caption underneath her photo.

I leaned closer, blinking back tears as I read. "Mary Carlson was struck by a car exiting New Hope's orphanage on July 25th. Police are not charging the driver, Michael Hope, stating that it was a tragic accident. Please note, Carlsons' Diner is closed until further notice."

Things must've been really bad for the Carlsons for them to just close up their restaurant like that. They'd never been closed a day in all the time I'd lived there. I scrolled ahead, looking for news about when they'd reopened, but I didn't see anything. And I didn't see any other stories about the orphanage. I left the library with no new information about Wren or where he might be. My heart felt heavier with each dead end.

I'd been doing so much investigating, I missed lunch, and I didn't get over to the Finest until the afternoon. Thank goodness lots of people were already working. Some were painting murals on new sections of fence. Others were making a huge robot sculpture out of soda cans. Jenny Gray was there, too, painting one of the bedrooms purple. Now that her own color was blooming brighter, I could see she was wearing purple, too.

"I'm going to fill this room with purple things!" she said. "Spread the word, anyone with something purple can put it on display here."

"I will!" Now that I could see it, I was really impressed by her colors. Everything she wore was a nice, glowing purple. "Say, did you know any of the kids who used to live here?"

"Went to school with a few of them," she said. "But I didn't know any of them well." She was much older than Joe, so she couldn't have gone to school with him and Wren.

"Any of them still live in town? Besides Joe?"

She stopped to think. "I don't think so."

"Someone named Wren?"

She thought for a minute. "Never knew anyone by that name."

Ugh. The Finest was coming right along, but I was getting nowhere in my search for Wren. And I didn't want to chase away Joe with more of my questions.

Parker and Chase spent most of the afternoon unloading Grauntie's snow globes in one of the second floor bedrooms, then going back to Grauntie's to bring back more. Took us five trips, and then I helped organize the snow globes in the room. Some were holiday-themed, and some had the names and landmarks of different cities inside.

Mr. Gaiser came up with the idea to build shelves in one room to display them all, and even donated supplies from his store to make them. "Once I'm finished with these, we can work on that welding project of yours, Penny."

When I went outside, a line of kids was filing into the building. Some were in my grade; others were older, some younger. I held up my hand, and the boy at the front of the pack came my way. The other kids followed. Must have been a dozen of them.

"We wanted to see if it was true that you were fixing this place up," the kid said. "I'm Nick."

I recognized him from school, but he was a few years older than me. "I'm Penny. And we are. Hopefully we can find a new buyer and finally open it."

Nick scratched his head, which sported the last-all-summer-long buzz cut most of the boys around the town had. "Can we help?"

"Sure, since you're offering. You can choose something from my trading cart in return at the end of the day." The cart was still nearly full. Most people working on the Finest never took anything, even when I told them to. I wasn't breaking Mama's rules accepting help, since at least I'd offered something in trade. I turned around, looking for a job twelve kids could do. The bottles and caps around Carly glowed and shook, and I knew that's where I should send them. "You can go work with Carly." Her soda cap mural was turning out real nice, with a big butterfly floating among my soda bottle flowers. Her mom had even joined her to help out. It was nice to see the two of them smiling and laughing.

Joe's tree house was taking shape, with the platform of the house coming to life around the trunk. He was taking a break, drinking a soda and looking up at the tree. All by himself, of course. No one ever seemed to talk to him—but at least no one was giving him a hard time.

I walked over. "Need any help?"

"Oh, I could use help, but I'm not letting a kid use power tools." He grinned.

"Too bad Wren wasn't here. I'm sure he'd be a big help." I waited, hoping he'd give me some more information.

"He certainly would."

"I can't understand what two people could fight over that would end a friendship forever." I crossed my fingers.

He said nothing.

"Did you guys beat each other up or something?" I asked.

He shook his head. "No. It wasn't anything like that." He tossed his soda can on the ground and looked up at the sky. "I figure you're going to pester me about this until I tell you." He waited a moment, and his shoulders slumped. Then he sighed. "We got in a fight about your mom."

I sucked in a breath. "So they *did* know each other." I ran my hands through my hair. This was like changing a question mark to a period. To an exclamation mark! Mama knew Wren? Mama knew Wren. Mama knew Wren! Wren, with freckles like mine. "But what could've been bad enough for him to just leave? Did you like her, too?"

He shook his head. "No. That wasn't it." He kicked at a stone in the grass. His face looked pained, and I hated putting him through this. But I had to know.

"What happened, then?"

"It doesn't matter what the fight was about. I just thought you'd like to hear that he did know your mom. Seems real important to you."

"Thank you. It's more important than anything."

It was a lot more than I'd expected to learn. And it was probably the most proof I'd ever get that Wren was my daddy. That had to be good for something.

That news took up most of the space in my mind for the rest of the afternoon. I didn't get much done. I wandered around the site, wondering which trees Wren had climbed. Which corners of the yard he'd sat in with a book. But most of all, I wondered where he was now.

At the end of the day, I went inside to inspect what was happening there, and even more people had taken on rooms upstairs: one had become a showcase for old toys, one was filled with rainbow murals and knickknacks, and one was taking on the form of a library with loads of books on the shelves already. It wasn't even my project anymore. It was coming alive on its own. I swear, it seemed like the building sighed, content with finally being tended to.

Work wrapped up by dinnertime, with everyone promising to come back the next day. Some folks said they'd be bringing friends or relatives with them. I wondered if the whole population of New Hope could fit in the lot, 'cause it seemed like that's where things were headed.

Parker and I walked home, and he didn't say much along the way.

"Joe told me he and Wren stopped talking because they got in a fight over Mama," I told him. "Wren knew her. But after the fight, Wren disappeared, and Joe never talked to him again."

"So he left Mama. That's another reason I don't ever want to meet him," Parker said.

How could the two of us have such different ideas about finding Wren? We were twins. I raised my voice. "You're being selfish, not trying to find him."

He tipped up his chin and crossed his arms. "You're being bossy and mean."

My jaw dropped, then I snapped it shut and looked away.

We walked on, saying nothing, occasionally shooting mean glances at each other. My anger felt like a pot starting to bubble up and boil. When we got home, we silently stashed the trading cart behind the shed.

I shook my finger, ready to start arguing again, when I heard a strange noise. A moan.

"Children, help!"

It was Grauntie!

CHAPTER 15

We ran to the house, where we found Grauntie lying at the bottom of the stairs, curled up on the concrete walkway.

I knelt beside her. "Are you okay?" I helped her slowly sit up.

"I've been lying here for hours. Yelled like the dickens, but your Uncle Jake didn't hear me." She touched her head and winced. Dried blood covered her forehead.

Parker charged up the stairs into the house.

"What happened?" I asked her.

"I . . . I grabbed the railing and just tumbled down the stairs. Then I couldn't seem to get up."

I looked up the stairs. The railing was hanging loose where we had glued it to the house. My heart felt like a hunk of lead. This was my fault. The glue didn't fix the railing. "I'll call for help."

I ran inside for the phone. Parker was standing with it in the hall already, and he handed it to me, stretching the cord out. I looked at the emergency numbers Grauntie had listed by the dial before we even came to live with her. With trembling fingers, I called the fire station. "This is Penny Porter, and my Grauntie needs an ambulance."

After they promised to send one out right away, I tried my best not to think about the doom painting. Seemed like this accident was exactly the kind of curse those paintings brought about. Losing Grauntie was far worse than me getting stuck in a tree.

I busied myself getting Grauntie water and an aspirin. Then I brought her a cool cloth and covered her with a blanket. What else could I do? She gripped my hand while we waited for help.

"You'll be okay. Everything will be all right," I told her, again and again. But to be honest, I was reassuring myself, too. I didn't want Grauntie to be hurt. And I didn't want her to leave. What would we do without her? Here I'd been doing everything to keep the three of us together, and I'd ruined it because I wouldn't ask someone to fix the darn railing. But I wasn't supposed to ask for help. I had to be able to do things on my own. To not be a burden or a bother.

My heart skipped a few beats as I wondered what would happen to me and Parker once they wheeled Grauntie into the ambulance. And where was the ambulance, anyway? The fire department in town had one. Why was it taking so long?

I tried to keep calm and remember that I'd put Clara Barton on my family tree a while back. She was a nurse in the Civil War. People called her the "Angel of the Battlefield." After the war, she founded the American Red Cross, so since I was related to her, that meant I had some caretaking skills in me. I could handle this. I gripped Grauntie's hand. *I am the descendant of a great caretaker,* I told myself as we waited.

When the ambulance finally came, a sheriff's deputy was there, too, and the mayor! My knees knocked. Were they going to put us in jail since we had no one to watch us? Was I in trouble for not getting someone proper to fix the railing?

While the ambulance crew checked out Grauntie, Miss Meriwether led me and Parker inside and sat on the couch, patting the seat next to her.

We sat nervously on either side of her. It was way worse than being called to the principal's office for chattering during class.

"I heard the call on the fire scanner, and I was worried. I know it's just the three of you here. I wanted to be sure you were okay," the mayor said. "I don't know the extent of your Grauntie's injuries, but I'm sure she's going to be in the hospital for a bit."

"And what about us?" I asked, bracing myself for the next part.

"Is there anywhere you can stay for a while?" Miss Meriwether asked. "Any nearby kin?"

I pressed my eyes closed and shook my head. "Not that I know of. Not anyone who hasn't already decided they can't handle us."

"Please don't send us to jail," Parker said. "I bet jail food is horrible."

Miss Meriwether laughed softly. "That's not going to happen. Just let me make a few calls." She stood and walked to the kitchen.

I went outside to see how Grauntie was doing. "Is she going to be all right?" I asked the ambulance crew.

"We won't know until we do some x-rays," one of the guys said.

I walked over to Grauntie and I looped my hands behind my back. "Get better soon, Grauntie. Please. You have to."

"I will, Penny. You two stay out of trouble. Mind Uncle Jake while I'm gone. Can you find my pocketbook?"

"Okay." I went back inside, found her purse on the kitchen table, and brought it to her. Then I went inside and sat on the couch with Parker. We looked at each other. "Sorry we were fighting," I said.

He nodded. From the wrinkle on his forehead, I knew he was wondering if now was the time to pack up the cart and head for the mountains. I shook my head. His shoulders slumped, probably in relief. Even though he said it would be a fun adventure, I knew he wouldn't be too keen on the idea of living in the woods. Sweets didn't grow on trees; nuts and berries did, and he'd told me more than once he wasn't fond of squirrel food.

Miss Meriwether came back and knelt in front of us. "The Carlsons said they'd be happy to come here and stay with you until your Grauntie's back. Since they previously went through foster care training, the people from social services said it would be okay for them to stay with you for a while. Sound good?"

"The Carlsons were foster parents before?" My heart

warmed up with that news. Not that I'd ever ask them to take us in for good. That would be begging to be loved. It was just nice to know good folks like the Carlsons were in the system.

"The Carlsons can come here, for sure." Parker's eyes popped open wide and he nodded like his neck was a spring. "Can they bring pie?"

Miss Meriwether laughed. "I'll ask. Okay with you, Penny?"

I crossed my arms, not knowing how to feel. Mrs. Carlson would probably try hugging us to death. "That'll be fine," I said, only because I couldn't think of any other options.

CHAPTER 16

The Carlsons showed up an hour later with suitcases and stacks of takeout containers. The smell of that good food almost brought me to tears.

"I don't know if you two are hungry, but I've found a full stomach always helps make sense of a bad situation," Mrs. Carlson said.

"You two doing all right?" Mr. Carlson asked. "That must've been scary for you." His calm, deep voice settled over me like a cozy blanket.

I nodded. "We're fine. Thanks."

"Did you bring pie? We'll be more fine if you brought pie." Parker swooped his tongue over his lower lip.

Mrs. Carlson laughed. "We brought pie, and all sorts of goodies. We'll sit down and eat soon." She walked over to the front window and opened the curtains. The sun was sliding down the sky, making the clouds glow pink. Grauntie never opened the curtains.

"I'm not sure how we're going to pay you back for your help," I said. "I suppose I could make loads of tin can critters."

Mrs. Carlson squeezed my shoulder. "There is no need for that. We're happy to be here with you."

"I didn't know you guys used to be foster parents," I said. "But how come you're not anymore?"

Mrs. Carlson looked at Mr. Carlson, and he lowered his eyes, like something was real interesting on the floor.

"It just didn't work out," Mrs. Carlson said. "It wasn't right for us."

Now I looked down at the floor. "I see. Guess it would be awful hard."

"But we are happy to be with you two for a short while," Mr. Carlson said. "Does your Grauntie have a radio?" He looked around the living room.

"I've never heard her play one," I said. "She just watches TV."

But Mr. Carlson knelt in front of a piece of furniture I had thought was just a big stand covered with knick-knacks. He opened the doors and found the controls to a radio. He twisted a knob and turned on some music. Then he fiddled around with another knob until he found what he was looking for.

It was instruments only, like nothing I'd ever heard. "What is that?" I asked.

"Jazz," Mr. Carlson said, closing his eyes and smiling.

"Mr. Carlson's a distant relation to Duke Ellington," Mrs. Carlson explained, as she found the plates and started setting the table for dinner.

"Who's that?" Parker asked.

"He was born a grandson of slaves, and became one of the greatest jazz musicians this country has ever seen," Mr. Carlson explained. He pulled a harmonica out of his pocket and started playing along to the song on the radio, his eyes closed, his body swaying like he was making magic, not music.

I worried Parker might be bothered by the sound, but he was clapping and bopping to the beat.

"Mr. Carlson's certainly got a drop or two of Duke's blood in him, that's for sure," his wife said. "Mary did, too. She was amazing on the piano."

I nodded. That's exactly the sort of thing I wish I knew about myself. Maybe there was a famous musician in my father's family and I was throwing away a perfectly good gift by not taking any lessons. But how would I ever know? I sat there, thinking about family and letting myself get lost in the song.

"I've got dinner set out on the table," Mrs. Carlson announced, after a bit. "You all come sit down now."

Mr. Carlson put his harmonica back in his pocket and sat at the table. Parker and I followed.

The table was set with plates and napkins and glasses. Usually we just ate out of our takeout containers, or at the couch. A pair of candles was even glowing bright at the center of the table, like it was a special night.

Mr. Carlson bowed his head and closed his eyes. "Dear Lord, we thank you for this food and all your blessings. Please guide these children through this difficult time and place your healing hand over their Grauntie. Amen."

"Amen," Mrs. Carlson said.

And, quickly, I added a few thoughts to the prayer: *Please don't make us leave New Hope. Please help us back on the map in time so we can stay. Please help me find Wren.*

"Hope you don't mind that we grabbed some leftovers from the diner," Mrs. Carlson said. "We were in a hurry to get here." She passed a bowl of mashed potatoes to me.

"We love your diner food," I told them.

"Then you should see what she cooks at home," Mr. Carlson said, with a wink.

"This week I'll make us a big, home-cooked dinner,"

Mrs. Carlson said. She slapped the table. "Thanksgiving, that's what we'll have. With turkey and all the trimmings. And we'll give thanks for all our blessings."

"Yum!" Parker said. "Pumpkin pie."

Parker and I hadn't had a proper Thanksgiving dinner in years, and Mrs. Carlson was going to make it in the middle of the summer for no reason? "That'd be real nice," I said, trying not to sound as excited as I felt. I scooped a lump of creamy potatoes onto my plate. The meatloaf was still making its way around the table.

"You sure had a nice turnout at the site today, kids," Mr. Carlson said.

"I'm surprised so many people want to help," I said.

"I'm not," Mrs. Carlson replied. "People want to do good. People want things to be better, but they usually wait until someone else takes the first step. And that's what you two did."

I was surprised Mrs. Carlson had something positive to say about the Finest. I thought she hated the place. "It was nothing, really." I felt dishonest, letting her praise me like that when my only reason for fixing up New Hope's Finest was a selfish one.

"I'm ready for dessert," Parker said, before I'd even taken one bite of my meatloaf. Then he burped.

"Parker!" I scolded. For a small boy, he let out big burps.

He giggled, and so did Mrs. Carlson. "My word, but you're a hungry boy," she said. "Help yourself to seconds."

Parker looked confused. "No, we can't have seconds. Need to save them for leftovers tomorrow. 'One less meal we'll have to make,' that's what Grauntie says."

I tried to kick him under the table, but he was too far away. So I glared at him instead, thinking, *Hush! We don't want them worrying that Grauntie can't take care of us properly.*

Slumping back in his seat, he seemed to get the message. "I'm fine," he said. "I don't need seconds. Grauntie takes care of us just fine."

Why couldn't this be one of the times he didn't talk?

Mrs. Carlson smiled, but it was a small one. "I'm sure your Grauntie takes care of you the best she can, but we're here tonight, and we'll be here cooking dinner, so we don't want leftovers, right?"

Parker grinned and reached for the meatloaf. "Right."

I gave Parker another look, and he put his hands in his lap.

"Is your Grauntie able to cook for you?" Mrs. Carlson asked.

"Oh, sure, lots," I said. "If we're not picking up dinner from you, she sends me to the grocery store with a list for all sorts of stuff." The music was taking a slow, sad turn, with a lone trumpeter wailing a tune.

Mrs. Carlson frowned as she poked at her potatoes.

"I like doing the shopping," I said.

"So, can I have seconds or not?" Parker asked.

I shot him my dirtiest, nastiest warning look. Course, he wouldn't meet my eyes.

"Certainly, dear," Mrs. Carlson said, while Parker loaded his plate with food.

"We're fine here with Grauntie, really," I said. "The three of us handle everything. We don't need any help at all."

Mrs. Carlson scrunched her eyebrows together and continued eating her dinner.

I stuffed my mouth with food, too, so I couldn't say anything else to worry them.

When everyone was done eating, I stood to clear the dishes.

"Sit, child. You've had a long day. We'll get it," Mrs. Carlson said. "We'll join you in the living room shortly."

I have to admit, it was a treat not being in charge of everything. I sat on the couch, bouncing my foot to the beat of the song. The setting sun shone through the window, making the room look bright and warm, different than I'd ever seen it before. With the music in the background, I felt like I was somewhere entirely different, not in Grauntie's faded living room. Surprising how the sound of music can change the way you look at a place.

When Mr. and Mrs. Carlson came out of the kitchen, Mr. Carlson grabbed her by the hand, and started twirling her around the room.

Parker yanked me up from the couch by both hands, and we bounced and jumped to the tune. Of course, we didn't look as good as the Carlsons did, grooving around the room together, but soon all four of us were laughing and smiling like the second-helping discussion had never happened.

After a few songs, Parker and I plopped into chairs, while the Carlsons settled on the couch. "Is there anything you'd like to watch on TV?" Mrs. Carlson asked.

Parker shook his head. "I don't know what's on. Grauntie is always watching her shows. And her shows are boring."

"So what do you kids do here?" she asked.

"Work on stuff for the trading cart," I offered. "Read."

"Why don't we read a book together?" she offered.

"Mr. Carlson does great character voices." She flashed him a smile.

"Oh, we don't have books like that. We've got encyclopedias," I explained.

"No children's storybooks?" Mrs. Carlson sounded surprised.

"No, ma'am. But encyclopedias are better. They teach you stuff. Oh, and I did get a *Great Americans* book from Mr. Hanes before he left. We could read that."

"We can do that later. How about we tell you a story?" Mrs. Carlson said. "Let's tell them about Charlie."

"That was your dog, right?" I asked. "The one who looked like the critter I made?"

"That's right!" Mr. Carlson said. "Oh, he had so many adventures, that rascal. There should be a dozen children's books about him."

So Mr. Carlson started telling us about their black Labrador retriever named Charlie, who was blind, but made his way around just fine. He told us all about the time Charlie brought home a baby bunny.

"Not sure how a blind dog found an itty-bitty rabbit," Mrs. Carlson said.

"Did he kill it?" I asked.

"Oh, no." Mr. Carlson said. "He kept it for a pet!"

"What do you mean?" Parker asked.

"We fed and cared for the bunny, and planned to let it back in the wild. But Charlie would sit by its box like he was protecting it. And one day, we noticed the box had been knocked over. We expected the worst. Retrievers are hunting dogs, after all. But Charlie hadn't hurt the bunny. He was napping with it! That little fur ball was all curled up under Charlie's chin."

"Really?"

Mrs. Carlson nodded. "We tried letting it go, but it would always hop back to the door, waiting for us to let it in. Darndest thing."

"No wonder you loved Charlie so much," I said. "I've never had a pet."

"I'm sorry to hear that. Animals are a joy," Mr. Carlson said. He told us how Charlie would play with kittens, too, and let Mary dress him up in clothes she sewed special for him.

"That poor thing was always wearing a kerchief," Mrs. Carlson said.

"Was he blind even when he was a puppy?" I asked.

"I don't know. We didn't have him as a puppy," she said. "We were going to the shelter to get ourselves a puppy when we saw Charlie. The folks told us he'd been there for six months, and they were going to have to put him to sleep. So we took him instead. And what a fine, fine dog he was. Lived for six years after we brought him home."

"That's the saddest thing, putting down a dog just because he couldn't find a home." My voice sounded thick, even to my ears. "I wish there was a home for every cast-aside dog."

My heart was clogging my throat. I guess Parker and I would've been put down years ago if we were dogs. I crossed my arms. "I'm going to adopt ten dogs some-day, when I have a home of my own. And not the pretty, fluffy ones. The dogs no one wants."

Mrs. Carlson smiled. "I hope you do, Penny. Now, why don't you get that book and we'll do some reading?"

I scooted to my room, enjoying how the music filled all the empty spaces in the house. When I had a house someday with my ten dogs, I'd leave the music on for them all day when I was gone.

I grabbed the book from my nightstand and settled onto the couch next to Mr. and Mrs. Carlson.

Parker sat on the arm of the couch next to Mr. Carlson, who put his arm around Parker and pulled him on to his lap.

"Where shall we start?" Mrs. Carlson asked.

"I'm reading the whole thing again. I'm up to Amelia Earhart, the famous female pilot," I explained.

"Oh, yes, let's learn about her," Mr. Carlson said.

I knew her story already, but it sounded more exciting with Mrs. Carlson reading it. I loved hearing about Amelia's childhood—how she went on lots of adventures with her sister, and enjoyed the outdoors. I'm pretty sure we would've been friends.

She became very famous in the early 1900s when there weren't many female pilots. She was the first woman to fly across the Atlantic by herself. Seems like that would be pretty scary. Then she tried flying around the globe and disappeared over the Pacific Ocean. I hated that part. She had a dream, and it didn't come true. Still, she should go on my family tree, I figured. *I'm the descendant of a famous pilot.*

"What an interesting life," Mrs. Carlson said, closing the book.

"This reminds me of our bedtime stories for Mary," Mr. Carlson said. "She loved nonfiction the best. True stories about special people and the things they did. We could've read to her all night."

I sat up straighter. "Those are the kind of stories I love!"

"It's interesting to read about the people who've built up this world for us," Mrs. Carlson said.

"You used to read to her every night?" I asked.

"Why, yes," Mr. Carlson said.

"So all your nights were like this one? This wasn't just special 'cause of what happened to Grauntie?" I asked.

Mr. Carlson squeezed his wife's shoulder. "We had a nice meal and music and reading every night. It was lovely."

Oh, did that make my heart hurt. This is what real families were like? This is what we were missing? I crossed my arms, and I knew I had a mean look on my face.

Mrs. Carlson set the book down and clapped her hands. "My, how time has flown this evening. I'd say it's time for you two to get to bed."

Parker launched himself into Mrs. Carlson's arms, and she hugged him tight, rocking him back and forth in her lap. I stood and took a few steps away from the couch. I didn't want a hug. Not after all the goodness we'd been sharing. It was too much. Knowing some families had music and laughter and candles filling their homes every night made me sad, 'cause we'd never had that.

And now that I knew about it, I'd be wanting it and never getting it. The Carlsons wouldn't be here forever. Grauntie would come home, and everything would go back to the same quiet, boring, lonely way it had been before. No stories or songs. No candles or second helpings. It was like living your life without knowing about candy—and then getting your first and last taste of chocolate.

I swallowed hard and said, "Good night." Then I dashed to the bathroom to clean up and brush my teeth before putting on my pajamas and diving into bed. I wanted to pretend I was asleep already if the Carlsons peeked in.

I was in bed when Mrs. Carlson knocked softly on my open door.

"Come in," I said gruffly.

"Is everything all right, dear?"

"Yes. I'm just worried about Grauntie, is all. Seems wrong for us to be having all this fun while she's in the hospital." It sounded like a good excuse. I wasn't going to tell her the truth: that I was hurting now that I knew what a family could be like.

Mrs. Carlson tugged my blanket up to my chin. "Well, don't you worry. She'll be back home shortly, and I'm sure things will be back to normal soon enough. I'm sorry if we weren't sensitive enough tonight to realize how you must be feeling."

"It's all right." I felt lousy that Mrs. Carlson had a hint of sadness in her voice. That I had put it there. "Thanks for taking care of us tonight."

"It's our pleasure. Truly."

That night, for the first time in a long time, I fell right asleep.

CHAPTER 17

I woke to the smell of something sweet and warm. I followed my nose to the kitchen, where I found Mrs. Carlson flipping pancakes on the stove. "I've got cinnamon buns cooking in the oven," she said with a smile. Bacon sizzled in a pan, too.

My stomach gurgled, and my mouth watered. That was like years' worth of yummy breakfast food from Grauntie. And Grauntie wouldn't have cooked stuff like that to be nice. She would have done it 'cause it was in the fridge from a trade. And lately, I probably would've done the cooking myself. I shook my head to clear it and sat at the table with a huff. I didn't want another bite of that can't-ever-have-it-again-chocolate. "Can I have cereal instead?"

"Of course, if that's what you'd like." She got out our only box of cereal—cornflakes—and poured me a bowl.

"I'll take what Penny doesn't eat," Parker offered, his

voice all helpful, like he was promising to rake the front yard.

I glared at him, but he wouldn't meet my gaze. He knew what I was thinking: that we shouldn't be enjoying all this, getting used to it. I stirred my cornflakes with the spoon, trying to stop smelling the wonderful aromas in the kitchen. Turns out, there's no way to stop your nose from working—unless you're willing to squeeze it closed with your fingers, and that seemed rude.

"Mr. Carlson's working at the diner," Mrs. Carlson said. "And I thought it might be time to see what you kids are up to at the Finest."

I dropped my spoon. "You're going to come to the Finest?"

She nodded.

"Really? Are you sure?"

"I want to see what's got everyone in town so excited. There's a change in the air, I can feel it." She smiled at me, and I knew my sorry, crooked teeth were flashing back at her. I pressed my lips together.

Once we had everything cleaned up from breakfast, we walked together to the building. Mrs. Carlson told us the names of all the flowers growing in the fields along the road. "And look at that beautiful swallowtail butterfly!

I haven't taken a good long look at all the beauty outside in a long time. I'm so grateful for this time with you two."

Parker reached for her hand. They linked their fingers together, swinging their arms as they walked. I pushed past them, walking faster and farther ahead so no one would go grabbing my hand.

When we got close to the Finest, Mrs. Carlson slowed down. I figured we must be near the place where Mary had died. There were probably kind words of comfort I should've been saying. I just didn't know what they were.

But Mrs. Carlson lifted her head, looked up to the sky, and let out a long, long breath. Then we walked up the driveway together.

She clasped her hands in front of her as she looked across the lot filled with new treasures. "I just don't believe it."

"Isn't it great?"

"It truly is. Greater than I imagined. The murals, the sculptures, and a flower garden!" She sighed. "I can't believe you all banded together to do this."

"Me neither. But there's still so much to do." I looked around, trying to figure out what would be the best project for Mrs. Carlson. The tires piled up by a tree seemed to be spinning, revving up to become something new. That was the job for Mrs. Carlson. I walked toward them. "Getting rid of all these tires is my biggest problem. I just don't know what to do with them."

Mrs. Carlson walked over to the pile of tires and ran her hands over them. She stepped back and cupped her chin, examining them. I wondered if her fingers were tingling with ideas. I was too embarrassed to ask though. Maybe that only happened to me—like how I saw people in shades.

She turned to me. "I've got some ideas for these. Mind if I try a few things?"

"Sure! What are you thinking about?"

She tapped a finger against her nose. "Chairs, to start with. We can stack two on top of each other and paint them up nice and pretty. Use one for a back. I can even sew some cushions and attach legs. Some other ideas are niggling at my brain, working their way up."

"Give it time; they'll come," I said. "That's how it works for me."

She set her hand on my shoulder. "There's just something about being up here in the midst of all this . . . this . . . busyness and excitement. I'm so glad I came."

"Me, too," I told her. She felt it. She felt that energy coming back to life here!

I left Mrs. Carlson looking at the tires, and headed over to the tree where Joe was working. The tree house was complete now, and he was working on the stairs.

I waved to him, and he climbed down his ladder.

"Penny, just in time. I could use a break." He grabbed a soda from a red cooler at the base of the tree, and handed me one, too.

"Looks really good." I paused. "Do you think Wren would be happy with how it's turning out?"

"I do. We sketched quite a few plans for tree houses, and this is quite similar to the design that was our favorite."

A warm feeling filled me. "Maybe he's an architect now, making important buildings all around the world."

"Maybe," Joe said softly.

"Penny!" Miss Meriwether was walking up the driveway, waving to me.

"I gotta go!" I hurried over.

"Your Grauntie is going to be fine," Miss Meriwether said.

Relief whooshed through me. "Thank goodness."

"She injured her shoulder and hip, but they aren't broken. But she'll be coming home in a few days with an aide who'll stay with her for a few weeks. After that, though . . ."

"We'll be there. We'll help like we always do," I quickly said. "It'll be fine. I promise. I'll do a better job." I crossed my fingers for good measure.

Miss Meriwether took on a serious tone. "Penny, it's not that simple. I didn't realize how bad your Grauntie's health was. How much you two children have been taking on yourselves to keep the house running." She shook her head. "It shouldn't be like that. And, well . . . there's someone you need to talk to. Parker, too. Can you get him?"

I nodded, but my stomach tumbled. I found Parker helping Mrs. Carlson paint some of the tires. "Miss Meriwether wants to talk to us. About Grauntie."

He dropped his paintbrush and raised his sunglasses off his eyes.

When we hurried back to Miss Meriwether, another woman was standing by her. That buzz that lived inside me kicked up a notch.

"Parker, Penny, this is Nancy Rydell. When the nurses at the hospital found out Grauntie's been taking care of you, they had to call social services." Miss Meriwether looked at the ground.

"The system?" I whispered.

Miss Meriwether nodded. "I guess you could call it that. My friend Nancy works for them, so I pulled a few strings and asked if she could oversee your case. You kids don't have anyone looking out for you right now, and I want to be sure we get the very best outcome for you."

"Thank you," I said, not entirely sure what that all meant.

Nancy folded her hands in front of her. "Children, given your great-aunt's health and age, continuing to live with her is not in your best interest—or hers."

The nervous hum was ringing inside me like an alarm. "It's fine. Parker and I are just fine with Grauntie. We can work harder. Do more. We didn't fix the railing the right way. It's our fault she fell, and I'm so sorry." We couldn't leave. Not until we got New Hope back on the map. That would keep us here forever—I just knew it.

The mayor let out a long breath. "You need someone to take care of you. Your Grauntie is experiencing memory loss. I'm sad to say, her condition is going to get worse. And what if she falls again?"

Parker leaned against me and wrapped his arms around my waist. I rubbed his back. "So what are you trying to say?" I asked, even though I knew.

We were getting bounced again.

"We need to find you a new home," Mrs. Rydell said.

I shook my head. "Mrs. Rydell, we like it here. We don't want to leave."

"It's more important to get you in a suitable home," she said.

"No, please. We need to stay here. Here in New Hope."

"Maybe a relative would be willing to move here for you," Miss Meriwhether suggested. "Maybe your Grauntie's daughter?"

"She already took us once, and she doesn't want us. Mama left us to her mama, but that didn't work out. And everyone else tried us, but we're just too much for everybody, I guess. I don't even know if there are any more family members to take us in." I bit my lip.

Parker buried his face in my shirt.

"Well, we can investigate that," Mrs. Rydell said. "We always prefer to place children with kin."

"And if you can't find any more family?" I asked.

Mrs. Rydell blinked at me a few times. "We'll have to look into other scenarios."

I wanted to cry. I wanted to holler, *You can't break us up!* Instead, I just nodded. There was only one thing I could do: make sure New Hope's Finest opened as soon as possible. I had to get New Hope back on the map. Otherwise, we'd be living in the woods—because no way, no how would we be going to a foster home. That, or I could find Wren. But I'd gotten nowhere with the search.

Then I had an idea. "Maybe *you* could try to find my father."

"Is his name listed on your birth certificate?" Mrs. Rydell asked.

"No one is listed under my father's name on my birth certificate." I swallowed hard. "But my Mama spent time right here in New Hope the summer before she had us. I think she met someone from the orphanage. A young man named Wren, like the bird. I think he's my father."

She nodded. "All right. That's not much to go on, but I'll see what I can do. I'll be in touch."

"And I'll keep you up to date, too, Penny." Miss Meriwether couldn't look me in the eye.

Parker ran off, I don't even know where, and I went another way, stumbling until I found a quiet spot behind the building. Big smiles weren't the only thing I hid from people. I didn't want anyone seeing tears, either.

CHAPTER 18

I sat behind the Finest, peeling long blades of grass in half, twisting them around my finger until it hurt. I'd gotten a doom painting; of course something bad had happened. It hadn't cursed me with getting stuck in the tree after all. It was something way worse. Why had I been so dumb to ignore what everyone else knew? The doom painting meant bad things were on the way. The doom painting meant it was time to set aside hope. No Hope, just like our town sign said.

I let that box around my heart open a bit so the truth could settle in. Holding hope inside you sure is a hard thing when there's no reason to keep it there. I was only eleven years old. Why did I think I could fix everything?

But try as I might to let hopelessness take over, I just couldn't. The fight in me wasn't gone yet. I thought about David Farragut from Grauntie's encyclopedia. He was the most famous Hispanic soldier in the Civil War. He was just nine when he joined the navy. Nine! When he was twelve, he fought in the War of 1812. He was in the navy during the Civil War and until he died. People still say his most popular war cry from a famous battle, "Darn the torpedoes, full speed ahead!" Actually, there was a bad word in his real cry, but it didn't matter. Maybe that's what I need to do, too—go full speed ahead. Don't give up. Maybe I had a little bit of David Farragut's fighting blood in me. He was going on my tree. *I'm the descendant of a famous soldier.*

And maybe, just maybe, if I got New Hope on the map, good things would happen to keep us here. Someone might earn enough money to take us in. Or someone new would move to town who'd want us. Or Wren would find us.

Once I wiped away my tears and boarded up my heart again, I went searching for Parker.

He was trying to juggle some soda bottles, acting like he hadn't even heard what the lady from the system had told us.

"Parker, we need to talk. Follow me," I told him.

He let his bottles drop and followed me off the site and onto the street. "What?"

I took a deep breath. "You heard what that lady said, right?"

He nodded.

"So *please*, try to find Wren. I'm not bossing you, I'm asking you as nice as I can. Just try."

He crossed his arms. "What if we find him and he says, 'Get out of here! I never wanted you two dumb babies'?"

I shrugged. "Then I'll punch him in the nose."

Parker's jaw dropped. "You'd really do that?"

"If someone hurt you like that, sure I would. I love you, Parker. And I don't want us to get split up. And if you love me, too, you'll at least try to find Wren."

"Maybe I'll punch him in the nose, too."

"Or maybe he'll be so excited to find out he has two kids just waiting for a home. He's probably rich and successful and lonely as heck and we could make his life perfect."

Parker nodded. "Okay. I'll try finding him."

"Really? Thank you so much, Parker!" I hugged him as tight as I could.

He wiggled away and sat on the grass in front of the fence. He closed his eyes. His shoulders rose and fell as he breathed in deeply. One eye opened. "Jenny Gray's purple pillow is in her linen closet under her grandma's old quilt."

"I'll be sure to let her know. Keep trying." I sat on the grass next to him, looking for four-leaf clovers. Figured we could use all the luck we could get, but I didn't see any.

Parker's eyes opened. "Mr. Gaiser left his keys at the diner."

"I will tell him to get a key clip and attach it to his pants. Anything on Wren?"

"I'm trying." Parker stood. Then he stood and slowly turned in circles, his eyes wide open and not blinking. He looked like he was trying to find his way out of a pitch-dark room. Then he froze, and he whispered, "Penny, I found him."

"What? Are you teasing me?" I asked.

He shook his head. "I found him."

I jumped up and pumped my arm in the air. "Woohoo! Where is he?"

He looked at me with wide eyes. "Wren is right here in New Hope."

"What? Really? Where? Let's go right now!"

He frowned and kicked at the dirt. "I don't know exactly where he is. Just that he's here. Somewhere." So Parker and I rode our bikes around town to see if he could feel where Wren was, like if we were getting hotter or colder in different spots, but he didn't come up with anything. We peeked in the windows of some boarded-up old houses, but it certainly didn't look like anyone had been living in any of them.

"It's getting late, and I'm tired," Parker said after we'd ridden around town a few times.

"The Carlsons will be wondering where we are," I said with a nod. "Let's go."

As we rode home, I wondered how in the world we were going to find Wren. Maybe he'd been living quietly in some hidden cabin we didn't know about. But if the Finest opened, no doubt he'd come out for a look. Then we'd find him, and he'd be so happy, and we could stay here.

Only, I couldn't wait until the July 1st map deadline. I needed to make sure New Hope's Finest opened as soon as possible. Before we got shipped off.

ｵﾋﾄﾄ

The search for Wren was stalled again, but work on the Finest was buzzing along. Mr. Carlson was working on the tires now, too, making a Loch Ness Monster sculpture. Carly and her mom were cutting up more soda bottles into flowers, while a few of Carly's friends threaded them onto fishing line to hang from a tree. Mr. Smith was stacking all the spare bicycle tires into a crazy sculpture that climbed toward the sky, while Mr. Gaiser welded them into place. Kids were painting lightning bolts and stars and patterns on the bikes Mr. Smith had fixed. Everything seemed to be humming with magic.

I walked onto the porch, where I found that someone had made a bench out of a headboard from an old bed. Chatter and laughter rung out when I opened the door and stepped inside.

This isn't even my project anymore, I thought. *I don't have to be here. All these folks could finish without me.*

I tried to figure out how to describe this place when I took out the advertisement looking for a buyer, but I didn't know what to call it. It wasn't one thing—it was dozens of things: a snow globe display, after all; an out-door sculpture park; a museum of . . . everything.

I climbed the stairs and stood in a bedroom, looking out the window at Joe's tree house. I wondered if this was the very room he used to stand in when he was a kid, imagining the possibilities. And here he was, finally doing it.

Kids stood below where Joe worked, gabbing with each other and shouting out questions to him. Even from where I stood, I could see him smiling. Guess they didn't know how spooked the adults were by him. I wanted to feel mad at him about the doom painting, now that I knew how bad it really was, but I couldn't. I'd seen the sadness in his eyes when we'd talked about them. He didn't like them, either. At least now that his paint was out of his house, he had no way to make them anymore. Too bad I'd had the bad luck to get his very last one.

Just before supper, we piled in Mr. Carlson's car to ride home. Mrs. Carlson had left early to work on our Thanksgiving-in-the-summertime meal.

"We have a few more days with you kids until your Grauntie comes home," Mr. Carlson said as we drove home. "Soon everything will be back to normal."

I crossed my arms and looked out the window. "No, it won't. We met a social worker today who said Grauntie's too old to take care of us. She's looking for a new home for us. And I can't imagine it'll be here in New Hope." I snuck a glance at him.

"Oh, am I ever sorry to hear that," Mr. Carlson said. "Are they looking for more of your kin?"

I nodded. "But I don't think there's anyone left willing to take us in."

"Hey," Parker said. "You and Mrs. Carlson take real good care of us. Wonder if we could stay with you?"

"Parker!"

"What? We like them. Plus they're good cooks," he whispered.

Mr. Carlson pulled the car over on the side of the road and parked it.

I gulped. Was he going to holler at us? I glared at Parker. "Hush!" I hissed.

Mr. Carlson turned around to look at us. He was quiet for a moment. "We adore you kids. Truly. In fact, we've talked about whether we could take you in."

"Really?" I could barely get the word out.

"Yes. But Mrs. Carlson and I tried being foster parents once before, not long after Mary died." He closed his eyes for a few moments. "As we told you the other night, it didn't work out well. We got so attached to the little boy that we were devastated when he was given back to his family." He sighed.

"Mr. Carlson, I promise you, no one will come looking for us." I wasn't begging him to take us. I was just stating the facts.

"The whole thing just made Mrs. Carlson miss Mary more. It launched her into a long sadness. Took quite a while for her to get better. And she still has her bad days." He shook his head. "She used to have the most amazing smile. Lit up a room. Reached the heavens with that smile. I haven't seen it since Mary died, and I miss it so. What I wouldn't give to see it again." His voice got low and scratchy. "I miss my daughter like nobody's business, but I miss my wife, too. The way she used to be. So I hope you can understand why foster care just isn't a good fit for us. Let's not mention this idea to Mrs. Carlson. I'm sorry, kids. I really am, but it just wouldn't work."

My heart fell. Even though I'd shushed Parker and knew I'd never ever ask to be part of someone's family, happiness had bloomed inside me, just for a moment, thinking about being part of the Carlsons' family. Forever. "That's okay," I said. "He was just kidding anyways. We'd never beg someone to be part of their family." I glared at Parker. "Besides, you guys are way too busy to take in two kids. You're right; it wouldn't be a good fit."

Parker let out a long sigh.

"That lady's going to try to find our dad," I said. "I doubt she will. Still, it would be nice to know something about him. Something about that side of the family, the way you know you're related to Duke Ellington, Mr. Carlson."

He chuckled and pulled back onto the road. "I'm real proud of that. I hope you find something out, Penny. I'd bet anything you two are related to someone real amazing. Someone real creative—like Mr. Walt Disney."

"You think I could be related to Walt Disney?" I asked.

"Sure do. Do you know he was fired from a newspaper? They told him he wasn't creative enough. And look what he went on to do. And I bet he didn't do anything as impressive at your age as fixing up an old, forgotten building."

I nodded, feeling good from his encouragement, but feeling lousy that the Carlsons had had a chat and decided they didn't want us. I wished I didn't even know it.

~~卌~~

When we stepped into the house, the most delicious aromas filled my nose.

"You're just in time!" Mrs. Carlson said in a singsong voice. "Turkey, dressing, sweet potatoes, cranberries, rolls. Mmm. Everything for a Thanksgiving feast."

"Is there pie?" Parker asked.

Mrs. Carlson came over and squeezed his cheeks. "There's lots of pie."

We sat down to eat, but the flavors didn't dance across my tongue like I thought they would. Maybe 'cause my brain was distracting me with a rainstorm of questions. Did the Carlsons really not want any new kids, or did they just not want us? Maybe if we were better, or cuter,

192

or smarter, they'd love to take us in. Maybe if I knew who we really were—who my daddy was and the great things he'd done—they'd want us. Maybe if we weren't mixed, things would be different.

I glared across the table at Parker. He was no help, inhaling food like a stray dog, chewing with his mouth open and burping. If he wasn't such an odd bird, they might want him and take me, too, out of pity.

Or maybe Parker and I just weren't family material, and never would be.

CHAPTER 19

I did my best to avoid being alone with Mrs. Carlson over the next few days. It was too strange now, knowing they'd decided we weren't right for them. Felt like I couldn't look her in the eyes. Course, she was nice as ever, doing all the work at home, and bringing trays of food to the site at lunch.

People would swarm around her and grab something to eat, then sit down to chat and visit while they ate.

But I noticed Joe never came over to join us. "Can I take one over to Joe?" I asked one day when she arrived with the food.

Mrs. Carlson looked at him standing by a tree, watching us all. "I'll take it over to him, dear."

"Thanks. He thinks no one wants him here. You don't feel that way, do you?"

"No, I do not. I'm happy he's helping. I don't know why we didn't all get together sooner and work on this place years ago. Should've done this the day after those crooks left with our money." She looked down. "Of course, none of us had much money left then. Or enthusiasm." She took a deep breath and smiled. "Good thing for fresh starts."

I watched her walk over to where Joe was building the tree house. When he saw her coming, he climbed the stairs up onto the platform before she could reach him. If only he knew how nice she was, he'd try to get to know her.

She stood there for a moment, then set a plate of food on top of his cooler of drinks and came back to the group.

While we ate, people talked and laughed and told stories about the old times, when New Hope really did have hope—when the town had a Fourth of July celebration with a penny carnival and fireworks. When people planted flowers in their gardens and brought picnics down to the creek.

I wanted Joe to be part of this happy talk, too. Would he ever feel comfortable around people in town ever again? Not just the kids, but the grown-ups, too? Would his wish that he could make things right with everyone come true?

After I finished eating, I checked out all the work

being done. Mrs. Carlson had come up with incredible ideas for the tires. One was cut up in a way to look like a snail. Another looked like a turtle. "You did these all by yourself?"

She beamed. "I got the ideas. Mr. Carlson did most of the cutting, and I did the painting. I've got plans for more tire animals. I was inspired by your critters, Penny."

I felt a blush burning my cheeks. "My critters are nowhere near this neat."

"They most certainly are. And I got to thinking: Why can't we have a salon after all? We're going to have tire chairs aplenty out here, if people want to sit around in the great outdoors reading or talking about books."

"I think that's a great idea," I said, and we shared a smile.

Mr. Carlson headed toward Joe, but Joe hurried inside the building. I watched Mr. Carlson turn around and head back our way.

Joe was being silly. I had to tell him not to worry about the Carlsons being mean to him. They were the nicest people in town. So I followed him inside and found him wandering around the big back room where the orphanage kids used to eat their meals. "Why do you keep running away from the Carlsons? They're not going to say anything mean to you. I think they're trying to be friendly."

Joe took a deep breath and let it out. "I can't face them," he said.

"Because of the money they lost investing in the Finest? Everyone is getting over that, now that this place is coming to life. You have to give people a chance if you want them to give you a chance."

He held up one hand like he wanted to stop me. "Penny, you don't know everything that happened here."

"I'm sorry. I just want to see you happy. And I want you to stop feeling so bad about what happened here ten long, long years ago."

"That's not it." He shook his head.

I put my hands on my hips. "Well, if it's not the money, then what could possibly be so bad?"

Joe leaned against a windowsill and looked out into the yard. "If it wasn't for me, their daughter might still be alive."

"What do you mean?"

He closed his eyes. He looked like he was in pain. "I had a dream before she was killed. In it, I saw exactly what happened. And when I woke up from the horrible, very real dream, I said nothing. I didn't warn anybody. I should have told them to keep her off her bike. To forbid her from riding it in front of the orphanage."

I set my hand on his arm. "It's not your fault, Joe. You don't know if you could have stopped it from happening."

"And I had other dreams like that. Dreams in which terrible things happened. And I never told anyone."

"Do you still have those dreams?" I asked, a little bit worried.

He shook his head no.

"Then what's done is done. But Joe. The Carlsons want you here. And so do a lot of other people. Me especially. I'd probably still be up in that tree if it wasn't for you."

He laughed softly. "Thank you."

I wasn't going to ruin the moment asking more questions about Wren.

~~~~

The next day Grauntie came home with a caretaker named Lonnie, and Mr. and Mrs. Carlson left. Which was probably for the best. We were getting too comfortable, too happy with the Carlsons.

But when they left, it was like the world had turned to

black and white. Grauntie had Lonnie close the drapes. She shut the stereo cabinet. She put away the candles.

Lonnie would be staying with us for a few weeks. She was nice and did most of the chores we used to do. But it was only temporary. Time was a-ticking until everything changed. New Hope's Finest was my only hope. And I still had some questions for Joe. It was all I could think about as I tried to sleep that night.

The next morning, I marched right over to the Finest, right over to the tree house where he was working, and just came out with it. I was running out of time. I needed to know more about Mama and Wren and where he might be. "Why were you fighting over my mother?"

He closed his eyes and sighed. He waited a long time before starting to talk, like he had to roll his memory back to that day. "We were busy making plans for our future. Everything seems like a dream you can just snatch when you're graduating, ready to take on the world. So we planned to go to college and start our own business someday. We also hoped that would keep us from getting drafted into the war in Vietnam."

"What does my mom have to do with it?" I asked.

"He didn't want to go off and leave her. He wanted to stay and take our chances fixing up the old orphanage."

He shrugged. "Course, I was mad as anything. It didn't end well between us. Like I said, he left and we never talked again."

I swallowed a few times before I could ask, "Did he know about us?"

He quickly shook his head. "He never mentioned a baby. Just that he was in love and wanted to stay here. I told him he was throwing away his life, throwing away our dreams. I asked him what would happen if he got drafted because he didn't go to college." Joe looked down, shaking his head. "But he reminded me that while the Clarks adopted me, and other kids had found new homes or foster homes, no one had chosen him. He was living on the couch in our basement. He had no one, and then he finally found somebody, and she was more important than anything to him. And if I couldn't understand that, he said, then I wasn't a true friend." Joe closed his eyes. His face looked pained. "Then he got into his car and sped off."

My heart was beating fast, knowing I was getting close to hearing the truth. "So what happened to him?"

Joe leaned against the tree and looked up at the sky. "He wound up joining the war in Vietnam."

"That was a long time ago. Where is he now?"

He didn't answer.

"Joe, where is he?" Even though I knew, thanks to Parker, that Wren was right here in New Hope, I couldn't tell anyone *how* I knew. It was just too hard to explain.

"I don't know. We never talked again. No more questions, please. I need to go home. This is too much hurt to dig up." He pushed himself away from the tree and hurried off toward his truck.

I sighed. What was he hiding? I stood by the tree for a bit, hoping he'd cool down and come back. But he didn't, so I walked around the yard.

At least work at the Finest was wrapping up; Wren would be hearing about it soon. Seemed like new things had sprouted up overnight. A garland made from bottle caps and plastic bottle designs stretched from tree to tree. That old rusty VW had been transformed into a stegosaurus. Someone had attached bicycle wheels to tall stakes and painted them to look like flowers with leaves. They grew up out of gardens Mrs. Gaiser had planted. The trees rustled, whispering secrets to each other, probably pleased with everything we'd done.

All the rooms inside the building were painted and decorated, each one different from the next. Even townsfolk who weren't working stopped by sometimes to check things out. And everybody's colors were glowing full blaze.

I couldn't wait for the deadline. We had to get back on the map now. It was time to place the ad looking for a new owner.

CHAPTER 20

I went to town hall to get help placing the ad, and the secretary sent me right down to Miss Meriwether's office.

She looked up and smiled. "What's on your mind, Penny? I haven't heard from the social worker yet, if that's why you're here."

I shook my head. "I think it's time to place an ad to find a buyer for New Hope's Finest."

Miss Meriwether walked to her window, looking at the building. Then she turned to me. "Sure, we can place it in a few different newspapers. What should we say?"

It was hard to come up with an ad since no one had ever been able to tell me for sure what New Hope's Finest was supposed to be. But I thought about Sarah Breedlove Walker, the country's very first female self-made millionaire. She had made her fortune coming up with beauty products for black women. She'd been real smart about marketing, getting ladies to sell her stuff door-to-door.

I'd been excited after reading about her, and I'd added her to the tree right away. I tried channeling some of her smarts now. *I'm the descendant of a great businesswoman.*

I thought for a moment, then snapped my fingers. "One-of-a-kind, enormous building right in the heart of New Hope, North Carolina, is now cleaned up and ready for purchase for what have you. Sound good?"

"Sounds perfect," she said. "I'll add all the other information a buyer would need. I'll let you know if we get a call."

"Thanks, ma'am."

"It's really wonderful that you started this all, Penny. I hope you won't be too disappointed if we can't sell it, though. I don't know if anyone would want to open a business in New Hope these days. But you brought the town together, and that's what's important."

She was wrong. The Finest was going to sell. It had to. "Just place the ad, okay?"

She nodded. "We'll keep our fingers crossed."

I raced to the front porch the next morning to get the *Asheville Citizen* and see the ad in it. I read it over again and again, imagining all the interested people who'd be sitting up in their chair right at that moment, reaching for the phone to make an appointment to see New Hope's Finest.

There wasn't much more work left to do at the site, but people were there anyway when I showed up. Some of the kids explored the tree house. Carly's mom and a friend sat on the tire chairs, drinking tea and chatting.

Around lunchtime, the mayor stopped by, all smiles. "Penny! We got a call. A businessman from Asheville wants to come and see it! He'll be here in two days!"

I jumped in the air and shouted. New Hope was getting back on the map for sure. I could picture the words in small black type next to a tiny red dot: New Hope. I closed my eyes, smiling.

But how Parker and I were going to end up staying in that dot was beyond me. Grauntie couldn't take care of us. The Carlsons didn't want us. Still, my bones were telling me once New Hope was on the map, we'd be staying put. Somehow that would conjure a solution to keep us here.

Once everyone heard a buyer was coming to look at the

building, the site cleared out. People ran home to cut their grass and wash their windows. Business owners swept their stoops and hung up welcome signs. Some even brought out flags and pots of flowers.

The next day, the one before the businessman was coming to inspect the place, Mr. Carlson set up a fire pit inside a ring of stones, and Mrs. Carlson brought hot dogs and hamburgers to roast over the fire. While we waited for dinner, Parker and I roasted marshmallows until they were brown and crispy.

Even Joe came, lugging along a watermelon. He'd shaved off his beard and trimmed his hair.

Mr. Gaiser patted the seat next to him, and Joe sat down.

"That tree house is something else," Mr. Gaiser said. "I've been wanting to build a new shed in my backyard. Maybe you can help?"

Joe looked shocked. "Yeah, I guess I could."

Kids chased each other in the dusk with sparklers, laughing and shouting. A few fireflies blinked in the darkness, like they wanted in on the game.

I caught Miss Meriwether's eye, and we shared a smile.

Mrs. Carlson put her arm around me. "This is how I always imagined The Finest would be."

I smiled. I never knew how to imagine it. All that mattered was that it opened. Hopefully, that would happen tomorrow.

The next morning, I put on my newest jeans and my button-up shirt.

I hollered for Parker to hurry up. Soon he was dressed in his best, too.

"Ready?" I asked. He nodded, and we walked into town.

But something was wrong. I could feel it. My stomach kept turning, and my hands shook.

The first thing I noticed was the missing signs. No flags were flying. It was like people had rolled the welcome mat back up.

"What is going on?" I wondered aloud.

Parker gasped. "Look!" He pointed at the Finest. And even though we were still down the street, I could see it.

The whole building had been covered with paint.
Squiggly lines of paint.

New Hope's Finest was one gigantic doom painting.

"No, no, no, no, no!" I shouted. "Why did you do that, Joe?" I ran toward it for a closer look. My heart felt like a stone in a lake—falling, falling, falling to the bottom. All that work for nothing. We'd never get back on the map now. Not with a building like that.

People would never forgive Joe. Maybe I wouldn't, either.

Parker and I trudged to city hall. We had to talk to the mayor before the businessman showed up.

The secretary, Mrs. Tuttle, gave me a sad smile. "I'm sorry, Penny. I know you had your heart set on that reopening. We all did."

I nodded, wanting to run back to Grauntie's and dive under the covers and never come out. To curl up and give up. But I couldn't imagine any of those fine people on my family tree doing something like that.

I put my hands on my hips, thinking about all the people on my family tree who'd run into roadblocks. I imagined them all around me, urging me on. *Don't give up! Fight the fight!* That's all this was—a roadblock. I wasn't ready to quit. We'd turned the Finest into something spectacular, and I was sure anyone with any sense could see beyond the painting. Besides, the businessman wouldn't know it was a doom painting. "We've got an appointment with a buyer, and we should keep it. Is the mayor ready to go?"

"Let me call her," Mrs. Tuttle said, reaching for the phone.

Miss Meriwether looked pale as she walked down the hall. Mrs. Tuttle was fading, too.

"Parker, why don't you stay here with me? I brought in some celebration cookies to share later, but I suppose we should just eat them now," Mrs. Tuttle said.

Parker settled into a chair and grabbed a cookie.

"Don't eat them all! We might need them later." I was holding hope in my heart as hard as I could.

Parker examined the plate of goodies and grabbed a few while I walked outside with the mayor.

"What a shame," she said, staring up at the wild, colorful building. "It's too late to cancel our meeting now."

"Everything's going to be fine. This is an incredible building. I bet he's never seen anything like it." I marched toward the Finest, and Miss Meriwether had to hurry to keep up, even with those long legs of hers.

When we opened the gate, Joe was there with a can and a brush, slopping white paint over the colorful swirls and squiggles in the bottom corner of the building. He turned to look at us, tears streaming down his face. "I'm so sorry. I don't even remember doing this."

I walked up to him and set my hand on his shoulder. "It's going to be okay." But it was hard to believe my own words. I'd learned firsthand that doom paintings were bad luck.

"The businessman is here," the mayor said, walking toward the gate as car tires crunched along the gravel drive.

I crossed my fingers. "Make a wish, Joe. Make a wish that this is going to work."

"Wishes don't work, Penny," Joe said. "I have a lifetime of proof to know for sure."

A man with thick, black hair and a dark-blue suit walked in with the mayor. He pushed his glasses up his nose with one finger. Then he stopped walking and put his hands on his hips, looking everything over.

He wasn't smiling.

"Penny, come meet Mr. Henderson," the mayor said. "Penny spearheaded the campaign to clean this place up. You should have seen the mess back here before work got underway. Nearly everyone in town turned out to help. She's a spitfire, this one."

My cheeks felt hot, hearing Miss Meriwether talk

about me like that. I walked over and held out my hand. "Pleased to meet you, sir."

"You, too, Penny," he said, gripping my hand. "This is quite . . . interesting. What is it, exactly?"

I took a deep breath. "Well, that's a mystery, really. No one knows for sure what New Hope's Finest was supposed to be. But all of us have worked together to make it an incredible one-of-a-kind place." My heart raced.

He nodded. "Electric and plumbing all current and up to code?"

"Yes. We had some folks working on that," Miss Meriwether said.

"The outside paint job was a mistake. We've got someone working on that right now. It'll be covered up before you know it," I said.

"Let's take a look inside," Mr. Henderson said.

We walked into the front room, which was decorated like we were under the ocean, with murals covering the walls, and real seashells stuck on them, too.

"Looks like a lot of recent work has been done here," Mr. Henderson said.

"We all brought our ideas to life." Beads of sweat slid down my back.

Mr. Henderson walked into the back room and scratched his head.

"We had a bunch of paint to use up. You should've seen all the stuff that was dumped back here, but we found a purpose for everything." I gulped. Mr. Henderson wasn't nodding and smiling and praising me like I thought he would be—like everyone else in town had done.

We climbed the stairs, and I admired the mural Carly had created around my spilled yellow paint. She had painted a sun shining at the top of the stairs, and the paint running down the stairs looked like the reflection over water. It was amazing.

But Mr. Henderson said nothing. And he was silent as we toured the rooms upstairs.

"This one's my favorite." I led him into the rainbow room. "Each room is different."

"There are two floors of bedrooms, ten on each floor," Miss Meriwether said. "Perfect for a hotel or office space. And there are four whole acres here, should you need additional building space or a parking lot."

We went outside, and I couldn't help but smile, looking at all our work: the tree house; the bottle cap murals and paintings on the fence; the Carlsons' tire chairs and sculptures; my giant critters. All the crazy wind chimes hanging from the trees.

Mr. Henderson frowned.

I cleared my throat. "You could change all this, of course, if it's not what you like. It's just better than it was with piles of junk everywhere."

"Actually, piles of junk would be easier to clean up than all this. I'm afraid all the changes and customization you've done here would just be too costly to fix to make this a viable venture. Do you have any idea how much it would cost just to remove the paint from the brick building? And to dismantle the tree house?" He shook his head. "I'm sorry. This isn't going to work for me. Thank you for your time."

Miss Meriwether nodded sadly and walked him to his car, while I stood there, my eyes hot with tears and my throat tight.

Joe stopped painting and came over to me. "I'm sorry. This is all my fault."

"No. It's my fault, Joe. We turned this into something no one will ever want, and . . ." I sucked in a deep breath, my voice trembling. "It was all my idea." What had seemed magical to me just a few moments ago now looked like a ridiculous jumble of nonsense. No one would want it now. Mr. Henderson was right. How had the buzzing in my head and the humming in my bones been so wrong?

I wrung my hands in front of me, wishing someone would wrap their arms around me and tell me everything was going to be okay. Wishing Mama was still alive so I could bury my face in the crook of her neck. Wishing I wasn't all alone trying to figure everything out for me and Parker.

But like Joe said, wishes don't come true.

Carly and her mother walked through the gate, followed by Chase and Mr. Smith. No one said a word. I watched their colors drain as they stood there.

I didn't know what to say. I didn't know what to do.

Miss Meriwether returned and set her hands on my shoulders. "Maybe we'll get another interested party who can see beyond all the objections Mr. Henderson raised."

I nodded, but I knew she was wrong. This place was special only to us, and only because we made it.

"It looks a lot better than it used to," Carly's mom said.

"Even with the doom painting?" I asked.

She pursed her lips.

More people from town joined us, crossing their arms and muttering in sad tones.

Joe set down his brush and put the lid on his paint

can. He came over to me, his eyes fixed on the ground. "I shouldn't have agreed to work here. I should have known something bad was going to happen."

Part of me was mad at him for doing it, but a bigger part was flooded with sadness for him. "You don't know what your paintings mean. You didn't know you were going to paint the building."

"It's clear I make bad things happen. I should have seen it coming. I just should have known better than to hope." Joe sighed. "I'm going home. I'll get back to this tonight when everyone clears out. It'll probably take me a few days, but I'll get it covered in a coat of white."

I nodded, and he trudged off. I felt horrible now, for dragging him down here to work on this project and getting him hurt all over again.

More and more people came through the gates. Some just stood there staring at the doom painting, shaking their heads. Others walked around the site, running their fingers over the murals or examining the sculptures.

Still, despite all the sadness and all the fading colors, despite Joe's sadness, the air around New Hope's Finest seemed to buzz with a thousand happy memories.

And a thousand crushed dreams.

CHAPTER 21

I climbed the stairs to the tree house and curled up in the corner. I imagined my family tree folks up there, too, fretting and worrying right along with me. What would Martin Luther King, Jr. do? How would Thomas Edison fight back against this huge failure? It took him a thousand tries before he came up with the right way to make a light bulb. But fixing up the Finest seemed like more of a one chance deal.

I felt horrible. Because of me and this big idea, all of New Hope was crushed again, just like Miss Meriwether had been afraid of.

I looked down to the yard and saw everyone trudging down the driveway. This place was a heartache all over again. Maybe even a bigger one because we'd all worked on it together.

Guess I wasn't the descendant of an inventor, or a leader, or a founder. I was nothing but a failure.

"Why didn't this work?" I whispered into the breeze fluttering the tree leaves. "How can I make this right?" I closed my eyes, feeling the hot tears streaming down my cheeks.

The breeze got stronger, and the trees trembled. The wind whipped leaves from the limbs, blowing them up, up, out of sight. The sky darkened, and rain gushed from it. I hunkered down, waiting for the storm to pass.

It wasn't ten minutes later that the storm suddenly stopped, and the sun came out full force, like it never shines 'round these parts. I climbed down the tree house stairs and looked around the site.

Several of the trees were stripped bare of their leaves. The paint hadn't been washed off the building, but everything looked shiny and new. There weren't even any leaves or sticks scattered around.

I walked around, examining the sculptures, and a few more folks from town showed up, quietly walking around the site.

Tires crunched on the gravel driveway, and I looked up in surprise. A big white RV was making its way toward the building. A man in a tropical-print shirt and a ball cap stepped out of it, followed by a lady and two little kids. The man's eyes were wide as he looked all around. "What is this place?"

No one answered.

"There was a clearing in the trees, and I saw the wild painting from the highway. I just had to pull over and take a look," he said, turning 'round in circles.

I cleared my throat, which was still tight from my tears, and stepped closer to him. "It's New Hope's Finest." I tried to think of a word to add, but I didn't know what New Hope's Finest was. New Hope's Finest Place? New Hope's Finest Spot? New Hope's Finest Disappointment?

"It sure is fine," the man said. "Can we look around?"

"Be my guest," I said.

The lady with him smiled at us. "Is there somewhere to grab a bite to eat afterward? We also need to fill up the RV and grab some groceries. Any place in town to do that?"

The mayor was walking up the driveway, looking curious. "There certainly is," she said. "I'll be happy to show you when you're done here."

The two kids ran toward a pair of tire swings, while their mother took a closer look at the fence paintings. The man went inside the building, and soon called his family to join him.

Then two more strangers wandered in—an older man and a woman, looking at a map. "What is this?" the lady asked. "We saw this building in the distance as we were driving and had to see what it was all about."

"Where are we?" the man asked. "Looks like you're not on the map."

My shoulders slumped. "We're not. This is New Hope, North Carolina, and this is New Hope's Finest. You're welcome to take a look around," I said. "I'd be happy to give you a tour."

"That would be lovely. We needed a break from driving. Perhaps we'll get some snacks while we're here."

卌

And that's how the rest of the day went. Dozens of strangers spotted the doom painting and stopped by for a look. People from town were happy to give tours and answer questions. Main Street was filled with cars, the sidewalks bustling with tourists.

Folks from town were there, too. I saw Miss Meriwether swirling and twirling in the big front room, to music she must've only heard in her mind, 'cause I didn't hear any. Mrs. Carlson sat on one of her tire chairs, reading a book. Mrs. Gaiser wandered through the beautiful flowers that she'd planted.

Carly swung for hours on a tire swing. "This is even better than I imagined," she told me. "I *knew* it was going to be a giant playground."

Somehow, the Finest had become all those wonderful things everyone had dreamed about. And it was going to keep being those things—bringing new people to New Hope, maybe even bringing back people who left.

"Wow," Parker said when he wandered to the site. "The buyer opened New Hope's Finest already?"

"No. He didn't want it. Basically said we ruined it. But drivers saw Joe's painting and have been pulling over for a closer look all day." I sucked in a breath as something dawned on me. "Oh no! He's planning to cover up the doom painting tonight. We have to tell him not to!" I groaned. "His house is so far away, and our bikes are back at Grauntie's!"

"Let's borrow two of the bikes Mr. Smith fixed up," Parker suggested.

"Great idea!"

We ran back to the building where dozens of bikes were lined up along a fence, and we took two.

"What are you doing?" Carly asked.

"We have to tell Joe not to cover up his doom painting

tonight. All these people stopped by to see it. It's not a jinx. It's a good thing," I said.

"Can I come?" she asked.

"Sure!"

"Me, too," Chase said. Some of the other kids who'd been working on the site grabbed bikes, too.

Soon, there were almost ten of us zooming off on those old bikes through town, streamers flying just like I'd imagined. When we got to Joe's, we stormed onto his porch. I rang his doorbell while pounding on his door. "Joe, open up! We have to talk to you."

No answer.

"Please, Joe! You can't cover up your painting. It's a good thing. Wait until you hear what happened. Joe!"

The door cracked open and Joe's eye stared out at me. "What now?"

I explained how people had spotted his painting and drove into town for a better look. "It wasn't a doom painting—it was . . . a boom painting!"

"The businesses on Main Street are packed today!" Chase said. "It's so exciting."

"So whatever you do, don't paint that building," Parker said.

"But since people are stopping for a look, we need to make things official. We need to paint the final word on the sign," I said. "I don't know what to call it, though. It's New Hope's Finest . . . what?"

Everyone started shouting out different suggestions: Wonderland, Cool Place, Hangout.

Then Joe opened the door with the biggest grin on his face. "I know what to paint on the sign. I'll be right over."

We rode back to town, making guesses on what Joe was going to paint.

"I think he's going to pick mine," Parker said. "New Hope's Finest Extravaganza."

I laughed. "Not sure there's room for that."

"Mine's best," Carly said. "New Hope's Finest Playground. Because it's finally a fantastic playground now, with the tree house and the swings."

None of them sounded right to me, though.

When we got back to the building, strangers were still milling about, some talking about plans to spend the night in the bed-and-breakfast that hadn't had a customer in years. There were townsfolk walking around, like they had to see for themselves there were really all these people in New Hope talking and laughing and having a good time.

Then Joe pulled up in his truck.

"Oh, no, what's he going to do now?" someone groaned.

"Go home!" someone shouted.

I planted my fists on my hips. "Hey! If he hadn't painted this building, none of these people would have noticed it, and none of them would be here. He's going to finish the sign for us."

"That's true," Mr. Gaiser said.

People shut their mouths, and angry eyes softened, watching what he was doing.

Joe pulled the truck right up to the building and hopped out. "You ready?" he asked me.

"Yes. But what are you going to put on it? Because what is it, really? It's not just a snow globe display, or a dance ballroom, or a playground, or a salon. What is a name for all those things?"

People around us started chiming in with their own ideas.

But Joe just smiled and spread his arms wide. "This is New Hope's Finest."

"Finest what?" Carly asked.

"Finest everything," Joe said.

"What is?" I asked.

"This," he said, arms open wide. "All this. It's the finest thing in town."

Most people still looked confused. Then Mrs. Carlson

said, "He's right. This is New Hope's Finest. All these things we did together. It is what it is—our finest work. The finest spirit of our community."

"True. It was our finest thing when it was the orphanage, too," Miss Meriwether said.

It all made sense. It didn't need a name to explain what it was. It was what it was. "So what are you going to paint up there?" I asked.

"You'll see."

We all stood with our eyes to the sky as Joe went up in his bucket, paintbrush, and can in hand.

I couldn't see exactly what he was painting—just a few letters of it, like an N and an O.

When he finally lowered himself down in the bucket, we all stood there blinking at what he wrote. Then we cheered.

NEW HOPE'S FINEST IS OPEN

I shouted as I read the words. The Finest was open. It was really open! We all hugged and cheered and hollered. Sure wished I had some confetti to throw.

Somewhere on my family tree, someone must've had a moment of pride like this. I thought about it for a moment and wondered if this was how Booker T. Washington felt when he opened the Tuskegee Institute, a college for black students. He'd been born a slave and couldn't go to school until the Civil War ended. Then he became a teacher and was asked to create this new institute. Of course he did a lot more work than I did, but I can imagine he had the same feeling of pride when his school opened as I did, standing there looking at this new place. A place that hadn't existed until we all worked together and made it what it is. *I'm the descendant of a great founder.* I grinned. *And I am a founder, too.*

"Can you paint the name on the back of the sign, too?" asked the mayor. "That way more people driving by will know to stop."

"I sure can," Joe said.

"Does anyone have a camera?" I asked. "I need a picture." Once the map people saw this, we'd be listed on it again for sure.

One of the tourists had a Polaroid camera and snapped a shot. The camera spit out the print, and the lady handed it to me. As the picture appeared, I got goose bumps. It really did look amazing.

"Can we borrow four of these bikes?" the man from the RV asked. "We'd love to take a ride around town, get some exercise. Been cooped up in that RV for days."

"Sure thing. Those are the Finest's bikes. Anyone can borrow them, just as long as they bring them back when they're done," I said, making that decision on the spot. No one protested. In fact, several other people grabbed bikes, too.

The place was still packed with people from town, chatting about the day's events.

The mayor came over and put her arm around me. "I don't think we're going to find a buyer for this." She shrugged. "I don't think we want to. It's ours."

"Do you think people will forgive Joe now?" I asked. "That wasn't a doom painting. None of them were. They didn't cause the bad things to happen. I think they were warnings. A sign to be on the lookout for changes—good and bad."

People around us were listening.

"Maybe she's right," Mr. Smith said. "That old clunker of a car was bound to break down sooner or later. Maybe it just happened after I got that painting."

"And guess what? I got a doom painting from him," I said. "And look at all the good things that've happened to the town!" I didn't mention Grauntie getting sick. No, I was trying hard not to think about that. "In fact, why don't you all bring your paintings here so we can hang them up right in the back room. It'll be our very own art gallery."

A few hours later, folks were showing up with their paintings. Joe brought mine down, too. Mr. Gaiser hung them up for us, and people crowded around to examine them.

"I see a dog in that one," Carly said.

"My dog ran away after I got that," Jenny said.

Chase cocked his head staring at another. "If you look long enough, you can see a building here."

"My garage collapsed in a snowstorm not long after I got that. Maybe it was a warning," another man said. "This painting might've been a warning for me."

Joe smiled. Sure was a nice idea that his paintings might've been made for a helpful reason.

I pulled Joe aside and lowered my voice. "Joe, maybe your warning dreams found their way to your paintings. You said you had some dreams but didn't say anything," I said. "This was probably your way of warning people without even knowing it. You didn't make the bad things happen. You were trying to help. When you left a painting at the Finest all those years ago, you were probably trying to warn everyone that the developers were going to take the money. Everything you create has some of your intention, right? I think the doom painting on the Finest was a warning not to get rid of it!"

His smile bloomed, and he patted my back. "Kiddo, that's one of the nicest things anyone's ever said to me. I like that idea a lot."

There was a line of people out the door, waiting to take a look—people from town, and strangers.

"Where can I leave a donation for this wonderful place?" a lady asked. "Seems like there ought to be an admission fee for such an incredible attraction."

"You're right about that," said the mayor. "Be right back." Miss Meriwether returned shortly with an empty coffee can. It had a slit in the plastic lid on top, and a piece of paper taped to it that said DONATIONS.

Wren would certainly find out about all this activity and come check it out. *Please get here soon and find us*, I thought.

I was eager to write a letter to the map company so they'd have time to put New Hope on their new map. So I pulled Parker away from the refreshment stand someone had set up, and we ran home.

Lonnie had dinner all set out on the table, which was a good thing. We'd been so busy with the building lately, we hadn't had time for the trading cart or chores or anything.

"I need to get myself down to that old building and

see what all the fuss is about in town," Lonnie said as we sat down to eat.

"Are my snow globes there?" Grauntie asked. "I'd love to see them."

"They sure are," I said. "It's one of the most popular rooms."

"I'll take you down there before you—" Lonnie clamped her mouth shut, but I knew what she was going to say. She was going to take Grauntie to New Hope's Finest before she had to go to the nursing home in Asheville.

"Not tonight. Too tired," Grauntie said, yawning. "Maybe tomorrow."

"Maybe tomorrow," Lonnie said.

Parker and I looked at each other. We were both thinking the same thing: Lonnie was only going to be with us a little while longer. What would happen to us then? We still didn't know.

And that reminded me to get my letter written. "I'll be in my room," I said, pushing my chair away from the table.

I got paper, an envelope, and a stamp from the desk in the living room, then hopped on my bed. I grabbed the book on my nightstand so I'd have something to write on: *Great Americans*, the book from Mr. Hanes.

Dear Mrs. Sheila Blakeley,
Charter Maps Secretary,

Good news! New Hope's Finest in New Hope, North Carolina, is now open. (I'm including a picture as proof.) It's been attracting all sorts of tourists, so we should be back on the map because people will be looking for us now.

Thanks so much,
Penny Porter

CHAPTER 22

The next few days, more and more people came to take a look at New Hope's Finest. One day, I found Parker selling our tin can critters out of the trading cart at the bottom of the driveway leading to the Finest.

"Parker! Those aren't for sale. They're for special people. Like the Carlsons."

"I know, but we're going to need the money soon, don't you think?" he whispered. "When we go to live you-know-where?"

I blew out a long breath. My insides were still telling me we were going to be fine, but the facts just weren't adding up. No one new had moved to town. No one had asked about taking us in. Wren hadn't turned up. Even with all this good news lately, it was possible we'd be living on our own soon. "I guess it couldn't hurt," I said with a sigh. "I can always make more."

Joe's truck rumbled down the road, and he stuck his

hand out the window in a wave. He pulled up the driveway and hopped out. "I've got a project in mind, and I could use two assistants."

"Are we going to make a doom painting?" Parker asked.

I jabbed him with my elbow. "They're not doom paintings anymore."

Joe just chuckled. "No, but it is a painting project. You'll see."

We climbed into his truck, and he drove a ways—all the way to the highway.

He parked his car along the shoulder. "We're going to do something that should've been taken care of a long time ago," Joe said, grabbing a small ladder and a bucket filled with paint and tools. He headed for the sign along the highway that welcomed people to No Hope.

I knew what he was planning. "That's a great idea," I said. I was surprised how much bigger the sign seemed when you were standing beside it instead of driving by it.

Cars sped past as Joe set down his things. "Can't imagine why we ever let it stay like this for so long." He grabbed a can of spray paint that was the same color green as the sign and handed it to me. "Paint over the whole thing. You and Parker can take turns."

"Really?" Seemed like a pretty momentous occasion to entrust to the two of us.

"Yep. There'd be no reason to do this if it wasn't for the two of you." He opened the ladder and set it right in front of the sign. I climbed up and took a deep breath. New Hope was going to be on the sign—and, hopefully, back on the map—soon enough.

Parker stepped back, probably afraid of the smell. "Penny can do it all."

Joe held the ladder in place while I sprayed the paint back and forth across the sign. Good thing, too, because someone beeped as they drove by, and I got so startled I almost toppled off. I finished the whole thing and climbed back down.

"That's fast-drying paint," Joe said. "We'll wait twenty minutes or so, and I'll paint on the words."

"Do you think we should add 'Home of New Hope's Finest'? I asked. "Or is that not official?"

Joe grinned. "Sometimes it's better to ask forgiveness than to ask permission. I say we go for it."

We sat in the back of his truck while we waited for the paint to dry. I looked through the trees on the highway, catching a glimpse of the house Joe had built.

"I sure hope Wren gets to see the tree house," I said.

"Don't you think you should try to find him and let him know you finally built it? Maybe you guys can make up and be friends again. And maybe he'd be excited to meet us." I shrugged, hopeful.

"I wouldn't be able to find him. Like I said, we haven't talked since that day."

I nodded sadly. "But maybe enough time has passed that you should look for him."

"That sign should be dry about now," Joe said abruptly, hopping off the back of the truck.

Clearly, he wasn't going to answer me.

We followed him over to the sign again. With a stack of stencils and some white spray paint, he carefully added the words:

WELCOME TO NEW HOPE, NORTH CAROLINA.
HOME OF NEW HOPE'S FINEST.

Parker and I cheered and hugged. Then we gathered our stuff and headed back to town. I was like Milton Hershey, the founder of Hershey chocolate—who was certainly on my family tree since he had built the town of Hershey, Pennsylvania, just so he'd have a place to make his chocolate. And here I was getting our town back on the map.

234

Must've had some of his ingenuity. Plus, he opened a home for orphaned boys, and we had been working on an old orphanage. And the way Parker loved his sweets so much, well, that would explain where his sweet tooth came from. Not sure exactly how he was on my family tree since he and his wife couldn't have children, but I was probably linked to his uncle or something. *I'm the descendant of a great giver.*

We drove back to the Finest, and people were buzzing around the building, including the mayor. When she saw us she headed right over. "Parker, Penny, can you come to my office, please?" She wasn't smiling.

We waved bye to Joe and followed her across the street and into city hall. Parker and I shared a few looks. We knew what this was about. And it didn't seem like she had good news to share.

"Please, have a seat." Miss Meriwether closed the door to her office.

We sat and I bounced one leg.

She didn't say anything for a few moments. "I heard back from the social worker."

My stomach felt queasy.

"Did they find any family for us?" Parker asked.

"Did they find Wren?" I asked.

"I'm afraid not."

My throat tightened and I couldn't say anything.

"So, we're staying with Grauntie?" Parker asked.

"For a little while longer, until they line up new foster homes."

"Homes?" I asked.

"They're going to try to find a family willing to take two children, but advised me it's most likely going to be separate homes at first. From my understanding, it is difficult to find homes for multiple siblings." Miss Meriwether sighed. "But the goal down the road will be to reunite you."

Parker and I were going to be separated. We'd been together even before we were born, and now they were going to tear us apart? I couldn't breathe. I searched my brain for inspiration from someone on my tree, but couldn't come up with anything. I was all alone.

"We're really going to miss having you children here."

"There's no one here who can take us?" I asked.

"I've checked. It's a very big responsibility. I'm sorry."

"The Carlsons were foster parents once," Parker said.

"And they made it very clear they didn't want us," I said through clenched teeth. "Don't worry, Miss Meriwether, we'll be fine." I swallowed. "When do you think we'll be leaving?" I asked.

"Sometime next week."

That didn't give us much time. I had to talk to Joe. I knew he was holding something back. He had to tell me everything about Wren so I could at least find some of his kin. It was our last hope. It was that, or living in the wild.

CHAPTER 23

I ran to the site and looked for Joe, finding him over by the tree house. I hurried up to him, breathless. "Parker and I are getting sent to foster homes. My Grauntie can't take care of us. We have to know where Wren is. You have to tell us how to find him. Parker says he's here in New Hope. It's hard to explain how he knows that—he just does."

Joe's shoulders slumped.

"Please! Do you know how we can find him?" I asked.

And Joe nodded.

I froze. "Wait, you know where he is?"

"I do." His voice was scratchy.

I stomped my foot. "Why didn't you tell us before? It's really important."

Joe bowed his head, like he was ready to say a prayer. "Because I wasn't sure you really wanted to find him. To learn everything that happened."

I threw my arms wide open. "Of course we do! He might not even know about us. This might solve all our problems! He might be able to take us in. We could finally get to know our dad. I want to see him, no matter what. Please." I folded my hands like I was begging.

"Okay. I'll take you to him." Joe led us to his truck, but he certainly took his sweet time, shuffling his feet, studying the ground "Get in," he said quietly.

I climbed in, over-the-moon excited that we were finally, finally going to meet our dad. But I had to fight off those angry feelings, too, that Joe hadn't just admitted the truth when I first asked him.

We headed toward the outskirts of town, and I wondered if there was some house nestled in the woods that we just hadn't seen before. Joe pulled his truck into a church parking lot. Grauntie never took us to church, so I'd never been there.

I bit my lip. Wren was a priest? I suppose that would explain a lot. But I was pretty sure a priest couldn't take in two kids. Maybe he'd even get in trouble when he found out he had two of his own. My heart started pounding. "You're right. Maybe he won't want to see us," I told Joe. Man, would it hurt to see the disappointment in his eyes when he met us. "Maybe this is a bad idea. Maybe we should go back."

"I'm sorry. This isn't going to be easy, kids." He got out of the truck and waited for us to follow him toward the church.

I gulped, excited to be meeting our dad, but terrified he wouldn't want us.

But Joe didn't walk into the church. He walked around the side of the church, to the back.

"Where are you going?" I asked.

He didn't answer. And then I saw.

He was taking us to a cemetery.

"Wait." Tears filled my eyes. "So, he's, he's—"

"No longer with us," Joe said softly.

My stomach turned. I pointed a finger at Parker and sputtered, "You said he was here in New Hope!"

"He is." Parker hung his head. "I didn't know he was dead."

I shook my head. "No, no, no!" I dropped to the ground and ripped out handfuls of grass. "This isn't fair!" I wailed. "How many kids have a mom *and* a dad who are dead?" I pounded my fists against the earth. "Why doesn't anyone want us? We're not bad kids!" Everything was bleary as I blinked through my tears.

"I used to ask myself the same question as a kid. Why didn't I have parents? Why didn't anyone want me?" Joe set his hand on my shoulder. "There's no great answer for that question. Especially for you two. You're wonderful kids."

I sniffed as tears streamed down my cheeks.

Parker gently patted my back. "Remember, Mama told us life isn't fair. It's true."

Nodding, I swiped the back of my hand across my cheeks. She had warned us.

"I'm sorry, kids. This is why I've been so reluctant to tell you much about him. Because there was so much sadness to tell." He sighed. "I'm going to pay my respects at his grave, if you'd like to join me."

Joe walked down a path of grass between the tombstones. Parker followed and looked back at me. He waved his arm for me to follow.

My head was spinning and my stomach was turning, but I stood and trudged along, realizing no one had ever taken us to see Mama's grave. I'm not even sure where it is. We didn't go to the funeral, either. Guess everyone thought we were too little.

Joe knelt beside a small marker and bowed his head. Parker sat to the side of it, rubbing his hand over the words carved in the pale, gray stone.

I didn't want to look at it. I didn't want to see the words telling me the truth. "How did he die?"

"In Vietnam," Joe said quietly. "Not long after he got there."

I nodded and held back another cry.

Joe sobbed. "It still hurts so much. I didn't want to share that hurt with you. I thought it was better you didn't know anything. I had one of my dreams. It showed him falling on the battlefield and I . . . I had no way to reach him. To warn him. That was the last time I had a dream like that. Probably because they were useless. First Mary, then Wren. I couldn't save either of them."

Parker looked at me, then looked at Joe. "Did he know about us?"

"I am certain if he knew he had a baby on the way, he never would have left. To be able to start building a family of his own? It would've been his dream."

"So he didn't leave us, then." Parker nodded. "I'm glad I know that."

I got up the courage to walk to the tombstone and read the truth. That my Dad was dead. "Michael Hope, 1954–1972," I read to myself. "Michael?" I asked aloud. "Not Wren?"

Joe nodded. "Wren was just a nickname some of the kids had for him. The caretakers at the orphanage named him Michael Hope when the hospital sent him here as a baby. Named him after the town. He was one of the few kids that came there as a baby."

"Michael Hope." I mouthed the words a few times. "I know that name. Why do I know that name?"

I'd heard it before. My mind spun, trying to remember where. No, I hadn't heard it. I'd seen it before—in those articles I read at the library. I closed my eyes and could remember the words: *Police are not pressing charges against the driver, Michael Hope, calling it a tragic accident.*

I stopped breathing for a moment. It couldn't be true. It just couldn't. I couldn't even say the words at first. Then they came out in a whisper. "Wren was driving the car. The car that killed Mary. Our . . . our dad killed Mary Carlson." My heart felt like a rock sinking to the bottom of the world.

Joe blew out a breath and nodded. "That's why he left, went to Vietnam. He was so ashamed of what he'd done."

"Did my mama know?" I asked.

"Yes. She tried to stop him from leaving, but he wouldn't listen. She left town the day after he did." He sighed.

My daddy killed Mary? My stomach felt like a giant rock had dropped inside it. My dad wasn't a notable person. He hadn't done something great. He wasn't amazing or famous or brave like the people on my tree. He wasn't what I'd imagined at all. He'd done something awful. Something horrible. He killed Mary Carlson. He was responsible for the Carlsons' greatest heartache.

I am the descendant of a killer.

CHAPTER 24

I said nothing. I just ran. Out of the cemetery, onto the road to who knows where. I ran till the air was out of my lungs. I bent over with my hands on my thighs, trying to catch my breath.

Joe pulled up next to me and opened the door to his truck. "I shouldn't have told you."

I wiped my cheeks. "No. It's better that we know we are truly alone. No more fantasies about a great dad waiting to take us in." I climbed into the truck and sat next to Parker.

He patted my leg. "I told you not to make me find him," he said softly. "Sometimes you should listen to me. Maybe Mama should have put me in charge."

Joe dropped us off at Grauntie's. I was in a daze as we

245

walked up the driveway, but I noticed a long tube was propped up next to the front door. It was addressed to me, from Charter Maps.

My heart pulsed with the tiniest bit of hope. If we were back on the map, then somehow things would work out, and we'd have a place to stay here, even if our daddy was gone.

I popped the plastic cap off the end and slid the map out. My fingers fumbled as I spread the shiny new map open on the floor of the porch. My finger traced the space between Asheville and Winston-Salem.

No! We weren't there. New Hope was not back on the map.

I blinked a few times, like maybe I'd just missed it. But, no. New Hope was nowhere to be found. New Hope. No Hope.

I'd failed. I'd been wrong. I couldn't do something as great as getting my town back on the map and finding a home for me and Parker.

Probably because I was nothing like the people I'd put on my tree. Guess I was more like my daddy, who caused the greatest pain to the nicest couple I knew.

I shoved the map back into the tube and shuffled to

the trading shed. My plan hadn't worked. My daddy was dead. Parker and I were on our own.

But we would not be split up.

Parker walked back to the shed from the house. "What are you doing?"

"We need to get ready." I tried not to let him hear how upset I was. I was still in charge, and I still had to protect him. "We'll pack our clothes in backpacks, and use one wagon for blankets and pillows and books. We'll fill the other wagon with stuff to trade, and some of our tools, so we have to be choosy about what we're bringing.

"Critters, for sure. That way we can trade with the Carlsons for food if we run out," Parker said.

"Grab all of them. Let's see what else we've got." I stepped inside and looked all around the dark, little room. But not one thing started wobbling or whining or glowing. What was happening to me?

I reached out for a can on a shelf, and what I saw made me drop it. The color of my arm was almost gone. I was turning into a black-and-white sketch.

Slowly, I walked out to Parker and asked, "Do I look different to you?"

He shrugged. "You look sad."

"I don't look like I'm losing color?"

"I told you, I can't see that kind of thing."

I looked at my arm again. It was black and white. Hope was draining out of me. Maybe I'd be black and white forever. "Let's get our stuff together. We're leaving in the morning."

Lonnie was sweeping the kitchen when we walked in. "Shh, your Grauntie is sleeping."

"Already?" I asked.

"She wakes often during the night. Leaves her tired during the day."

I felt bad, knowing we wouldn't be able to say goodbye to Grauntie. We'd have to leave her a note before we left.

I stood in my room like I was saying goodbye to it, too. But it had never really felt like my room. It was decorated with someone else's stuff. Grauntie had been the nicest of our relatives, but no great memories would be left here.

I sorted through my clothes and chose four pairs of pants, three pairs of shorts, and six tops, along with underwear and socks, sneakers, and a sweatshirt. It wouldn't be enough for winter, but I'd figure something out before then. Maybe we'd head south once fall came.

I grabbed my *Notable People* book and the book from Mr. Hanes, along with my family tree. I looked it over for inspiration, and my eyes settled on Chief Joseph. He led members of the Nez Perce tribe in the fight against the US Army. The army wanted the land Chief Joseph's people lived on because it had gold. War seemed likely, and he wanted to save his people from defeat. So Chief Joseph and his people fled from Oregon to Canada, fighting US soldiers along the way, hoping to meet up with Sitting Bull and live there. He knew something about taking off for a better life. *I'm the descendant of a great warrior.*

But then another thought crept in, reminding me of the truth. *No, I'm not. I'm the daughter of a killer.*

Besides, they never made it to Canada, and Chief Joseph surrendered. "I will fight no more forever," he had said.

Me, too, I thought.

Not all stories have a happy ending.

༒

I set my alarm to go off before the sun rose. Lonnie usually woke at seven, so Parker and I had to be gone before then.

I took a nice, long bath before bed since it would probably be a while before I could do that again. Guess we'd be cleaning up in streams. The thought made me shiver.

I forced Parker to take one, too, and then we went to bed—though, as usual, I couldn't sleep. But at some point I must have drifted off because next thing I knew my alarm started buzzing, and I slapped it off before it could wake Grauntie or Lonnie.

I tiptoed into Parker's room and shook him awake. "Time to go," I whispered.

We ate cereal and shoved some granola bars and apples into our backpacks. We stuffed our blankets and pillows in garbage bags and set them in our wagon. Then I went back inside to leave a note for Grauntie.

> Thanks for taking care of us. Hope you get better soon. Sorry we couldn't say goodbye.
>
> Love,
> Penny and Parker

As we headed toward town, I decided we should get a few last meals from the Carlsons. The breakfast crowd was just starting to file in as I parked our cart outside the diner. I took in four critters, hoping for eight meals.

These were the last critters I'd probably ever give to the Carlsons.

Mrs. Carlson spotted us right away. "You children are here quite early."

"We've got a big day ahead of us, so we thought we'd stop by and get some food to tide us through." I glanced at Parker so he'd know not to say anything about our plans. "I've got critters to trade."

Smiling, she walked over. "You never run out of ideas, do you?"

"I guess not." It made me sad to think of everything we were leaving behind in the shed. Would I ever have the chance to make another critter again?

She took all the critters from me and spent a while examining them. "How could I ever say no to one of your creations? Come on up to the counter and tell me what you'd like."

My mouth watered just thinking of the Carlsons' great food. Was this the last time we'd ever taste it? "Four BLT plates would be great, and four of yesterday's specials—to go?"

"Wow, that's a big order."

"I know."

"Sounds good. That'll be coming right up," Mrs. Carlson said.

I took a moment to soak in the memories of the place. To memorize the red-checked tablecloths, and the creamers on each table shaped like mooing cows. I studied each tin can critter sitting on the shelf on the wall. Would anyone ever love my critters as much as the Carlsons did?

Mrs. Carlson came out with our Styrofoam boxes and set them on the counter. "How about a hug?"

Parker pushed in front of me and held open his arms. Mrs. Carlson hugged him, rocking him back and forth. "Bye," he said, his voice thick.

Then she turned to me. "I'll see you soon, Penny."

I walked into her hug, trying to memorize the feel of her arms around me, the way my head would fit under her chin if I really snuggled into it. But I still pulled away quickly.

"Bye." I grabbed our boxes and hurried out the door, pushing away all the bad feelings piling up inside.

Parker followed and, once we were outside, he helped me find a place in the cart for the food. "So, where do we go now?" he asked.

"I figure we can walk out of town and head into the woods." I sighed, looking up and down the street, deciding which way to go. "There's that creek nearby we could use for water. We'll have to make a shelter. Let's get going."

But Parker stood there, staring at New Hope's Finest. "It's too bad that place wasn't still an orphanage. Then we could stay there, and we'd never have to leave."

My skin prickled. He was right. We *did* belong at that orphanage. That's where we would've ended up, years ago, especially with our talents. A girl who could see people in shades would certainly have been welcome there. Nobody would've found it strange that Parker could find missing things. Maybe that's why New Hope had always felt like home. We were meant to be here, all along. "Parker, you're a genius!"

"I know. But, why?"

I shook my head, laughing. "We can stay there. In the basement! No one goes down there, so no one will ever know. We'll be warm at night, and we can sneak out when we need to. It's perfect!" I twirled in place. "Let's go to the grocery store and stock up on some more food before we move in."

After getting peanut butter and bread and cookies and granola bars and water with our ten dollars from the silverware, Parker and I untied our wagons, carried them up the front stairs, and brought them inside. It took a while to bring everything down to the basement, but we did it just in time. Right after we brought the wagons down, we heard footsteps overhead.

Half the basement was filled with mechanical stuff, like the furnace and pipes and boxes and cleaning supplies. The other half was a big, open room with cement walls painted white, though not a fresh shade of white. More like the color of lost hope. There were two doors along the back wall, one closed, one open. The open one led to a bathroom with a shower and several stalls. Miss Meriwether had said the plumbing and electric had been fixed, so hopefully they worked. I went to the closed door and wrapped my fingers around the doorknob, curious about what was inside. I felt a shock when I touched the metal and snapped my hand back. *What's in there?* I wondered, not ready to find out. This big room would do for now.

It was totally empty, but the gray cement floor was dusty, and cobwebs hung from the ceiling like decorations from a sad, sad party years past. Luckily, we found a few brooms and rags so we could clean up. No sign of spiders, bugs, or mice, so that was good news, too.

After shaking out a big tarp we'd found with the

supplies, we laid it on the floor and unpacked our things. We spread out our blankets and pillows for beds. Parker was hungry already, so we each ate one of the Carlsons' meals.

"What now?" Parker asked.

I shrugged. "Read a book. Draw a picture."

Sighing, he grabbed a book and sat up against a wall to read.

I looked around. It wasn't perfect, but we were together.

There were no windows in the basement, so we could turn on the light without anyone outside noticing. We left them on when it was time for bed. Even so, Parker snuggled up right next to me when we went to sleep. Just like at Grauntie's, I spent most of the night staring at the ceiling.

美

"When can we go outside?" Parker asked the next morning, after we had each had a granola bar and water for breakfast.

"I'm not sure. We don't want to get caught now, do we? We should stay down here a while before risking it."

I read a few chapters of *Notable People*, but my fingers were itching to create. Sure wished I would've brought paint or crayons. I only had paper and a pencil.

Parker walked the perimeter of the room, counting to himself quietly.

"What are you doing?"

"Counting my steps. Sixty-two, sixty-three. Trying to see if I take the same number each time around."

I wished we could creep upstairs and look through the building again, just to see everyone's creations. Seemed a shame to have something so wonderful right over our heads and not be able to enjoy it.

With Parker pacing, it was hard to concentrate on my book. Finally, he tumbled down onto his blanket and pillows beside me. "I'm hungry."

I looked at my watch. "Lunch isn't for another three hours."

His jaw dropped. "But I want it now!"

"Parker, you'd eat all our food in one day if I let you. We've got to make it stretch." I still wasn't sure how to go about getting more food once our supply was gone.

"I'm hungry," he moaned, carrying out the "y" sound for at least a minute.

"Fine. Eat an apple for now. But that's all."

Keeping Parker amused was the hardest part of living on our own. And that was after only one full day! When I wasn't reading him books or drawing him pictures, I closed my eyes and listened to the footsteps overhead, imagining the people who might be up there. I made up stories for Parker about who was visiting.

"Oh, my, these people sound like they're from Texas! I'm sure those are cowboy boots clunking. I'll bet they have a trailer full of horses and they stopped for a break. Betcha Mrs. Carlson will give them some carrots and sugar cubes if they stop by."

"I miss her." Parker sniffed.

"Well, we can't go saying hello now, can we? We'll get busted and sent off to foster homes. Or worse. Maybe we'll get sent to jail for running away."

He stood and balled his fists. "I don't want to stay here anymore. I want a real bed. In a house. With someone like the Carlsons."

I shook my head, and softened my voice. "They don't want us. Nobody wants us. Do you want to get split up?"

Parker crinkled his eyebrows and shrugged a little.

I swallowed hard. "You don't care if we're together? We're all we've got."

He said nothing.

Felt like someone kicked me in the shin. "You don't care if you never see me again?" I could barely get the words out.

"I do." He shoved his hands in his pockets and looked down. "But we're too little to live by ourselves, Penny."

I stomped my foot. "We're not! Look at everything we did at Grauntie's. And Parker, if we leave this place . . ." I swallowed hard. "I might never see you again."

He shrugged. "Or maybe you will."

"No. We're staying here." I shook my head.

He jammed his fists on his hips. "Why do you always get to decide everything?"

"I don't."

"Yes, you do. You make all the decisions. I'm sick of being bossed around. I don't care what Mama's letter says. I want to leave!" Parker started crying. Little hiccup cries that I knew would turn into sobbing—fast. "It smells funny down here, and I'm cold!" His voice was getting louder.

Oh, no. He was going to fall into one of his fits. Someone might hear us!

I grabbed his baby blanket out of my backpack and

took Parker by the hand, pulling him into the mystery room in hopes of muffling his cries. I fumbled along the wall near the doorway for a light switch and flicked it on, then closed the door behind us. Luckily, the doorknob didn't zap me that time.

He sat against the door, and I kneeled in front of him, stroking his arms with the blanket. How could I ever let him go to a home without me? No one else would know how to take care of him. No one else would understand his fits. No one else could look at him and know what he was thinking, like I could. He was wrong. We had to stay together—no matter what. I wrapped my arms around him, rocking him back and forth until he was calm.

He sucked in a breath. "Wow, look at all those paintings." He pointed behind me.

I turned and looked at the wall behind us. "Oh, my gosh." I stood for a closer look. It was entirely covered with artwork—paintings right on the wall, some of them right over other paintings. They weren't just silly doodles, either. They were really good paintings, of people and animals and landscapes. All different styles, so they must've been done by different people. Different kids, I supposed. The kids who once lived here. It reminded me of Carly's mural room upstairs.

Parker stood and examined the art, too. It was a long wall with dozens and dozens of pictures.

I traced my fingers along the cold wall, wondering about the children who had made these creations. And why was all this artwork locked up where no one could see it?

"Penny, I think you should come here." His voice sounded odd.

"Why?"

"Because there's a picture of Mama."

CHAPTER 25

I'd heard about people's blood going cold, but I'd never known what it meant. Now I did. "What?"

"Come look. It's her."

With a thumping heart, I walked over to the other end of the room where he stood. I sucked in a breath. At first I thought it was a photo. But, no, it was a painting that looked like a real photograph. In the painting, Mama was smiling, and her red hair was piled up in a bun on top of her head. And she was holding a young man's hand.

A man covered in freckles like mine. A man with brown skin like mine.

I looked at Parker, and he looked at me. We didn't even need to say it. That man was Wren.

I wanted to hate him, but I couldn't. His face was so young, and full of love and hope. He didn't look like a killer. He looked like someone who had no idea he was going to make a heartbreaking mistake. Like someone who just wanted to be loved. We had that in common, at least.

In the painting, Mama and Wren stood in the yard in front of the orphanage. Other people filled the background, and it took me a moment to realize that Mama seemed to glow. Wren, too. The other people in the background were faded, some in black and white. Some almost invisible. Was that just me seeing that?

"Parker, do Mama and Wren look like they're glowing to you?"

He studied the picture. "Yeah, they do. Guess Wren could see people in shades like you. So you're not the only one."

My heart swelled. Then I counted the freckles on Wren's face, one by one. One hundred seventy-two, some of them in big blotches like mine.

We were connected. The good parts and the bad. But the sadness of knowing what he'd done had curled up and buried itself in my heart. It would be with me always. And I wasn't sure I'd ever be able to look at the Carlsons the same way again. It was probably a good thing I wouldn't have to see them anymore.

I moved over to Mama's side of the picture and

traced my finger over her smile. "I sure do miss you, Mama," I whispered. It had been years since I'd seen that smile. "Parker and I have nowhere to go but this dank basement." A sob threatened to sneak up my throat, but I swallowed it back down. "Please, Mama or Wren, help us. Please show me what to do."

I sat on the floor for a long time, examining that picture. A part of me wanted to dash up the stairs out of the building and run right to Joe's house to ask him about it. But then we'd be busted for sure. Busted, and broken up. Then I wouldn't have any family at all—just me.

When I finally joined Parker in the other room, we didn't talk about Wren or Mama. We didn't say much of anything.

After dinner, we read for a while, and Parker eventually dozed off. I covered him up with a blanket. Then I grabbed my family tree paper and added a name over on my daddy's side: Wren. I curled up with the tree next to me and fell asleep.

"Penny, you can't stay here."

I jolted awake and hugged my blanket around me. A

woman was squatting next to me, about five feet away. She was black, with her hair piled on top of her head. She looked familiar, but not from town. "Who are you?" I asked.

She smiled. "I'm on your family tree. Ida B. Wells. And I know what you're going through."

I blinked at her. "You refused to give up your seat on a train, years before Mrs. Rosa Parks refused to do it on a bus." I remembered more of the story from my book. "And you fought hard to stop black people from being lynched, right?"

"That's right. But long before all that, I became an orphan like you. Yellow fever killed my parents and baby brother when I was sixteen, and my relatives wanted to split up me and my brothers and sisters."

I sniffed sadly. "How awful."

"It was. So I know your pain. And I don't blame you one bit for hiding down in this basement, doing everything you can to stay together. I had to stop my schooling to care for my siblings so we wouldn't be separated. But, Penny, I was older than you, and I had help from friends and family."

I looked down, not willing to meet the truth in her eyes.

"And now your family's here to help you," said a man. "You asked for your family's help, right?"

I looked up and nodded.

He was standing next to Miss Ida. He was black, with cropped hair, wearing a suit and a bow tie. "Who are you?" I asked.

"You put me on your family tree after a bad day at school. You figured if I could walk most of the five hundred miles I had to travel to get to college, you could make it through another day at New Hope Elementary. If I could open my own school, you could suffer through another day of fourth grade."

Looking down at my family tree, I scanned the names. "Booker T. Washington!" I looked up, and now there were more people in the room. Startled, I scrambled backward until I bumped into the wall. "I don't understand."

A black woman squatted next to me. "You wanted us to be your family, Penny, and now we're here to help."

I studied her for a moment. "You're the lady who invented all the beauty products for black ladies."

"That's right. I'm Sarah Breedlove Walker."

I squeezed my arms around my legs tighter.

"You're an inventor, like me," she said, smiling. "Did you know I was an orphan, too?"

I nodded. "Your parents died when you were seven." I looked around at all the people in the room. Parker was still snoozing away. "Is this a dream?" I asked. "Or are you real?"

Sarah reached out and cupped my cheek. "What do you think?"

I gulped, saying nothing.

Sarah pulled her hand away, smiling. "Life wasn't always easy for me, but I never lived in an old basement with no one to look after me. You can't stay here."

"I slept on a dirt floor as a child," Booker T. Washington said, looking around the room. "This isn't much better."

"But if we leave, Parker and I will get separated." A stupid tear slipped down my cheek. "He's all I've got."

Another woman walked toward me, and I quickly recognized her: Harriet Tubman. "I know it's scary," she said. "I led slaves north to freedom over a dozen times. It was always frightening, the prospect of getting caught. And this here is a perfect place to hide, like the stops I made on the Underground Railroad. But it's not a place to stay. Not for good, child."

I looked around at all the people filling the room now: Daniel Boone, Rosa Parks, Carlos Juan Finlay . . . I recognized them all.

I gritted my teeth, angry that they were right. We

couldn't stay down here forever. "So what should we do? Sit in the street like Gandhi so they won't take us?" I scanned the packed room looking for him. "Is he here? He's on my tree." I spotted him in the crowd, waving at me from the back corner. I waved back.

"You could do that, but ultimately you need a place to stay, Penny. A safe place. Maybe you and Parker will be separated for a while," Sarah said. "I can't promise it will be easy. I always had to take care of myself." She shrugged. "Maybe if I hadn't, I wouldn't have had the gumption to create my business. But you can't stay here. Not like this."

Sarah turned to Booker T. Washington. "And I need to thank you, sir. I read your autobiography, *Up from Slavery*. It encouraged me to lift myself up, just like you preached." They shook hands and shared a smile. Then Sarah looked back at me. "And now we're here to do that for you, Penny. You need to lift yourself up, Penny Parker, and leave this basement. You deserve more. You deserve what it is you want."

"What do you want, Penny?" Ida B. Wells asked.

I looked in her eyes and quietly said, "Mama told me not to ask for anything from the world. So I wouldn't be disappointed."

"But you do want something," Ida said.

I glanced away and rubbed one thumb over the other while turning the idea 'round in my mind. "A family. But that's not going to happen."

Booker T. Washington rubbed his chin. "Not squatting down here, it won't."

"You're the descendant of explorers and leaders and inventors and great people," George Washington Carver said. "We all had to reach down deep to find the courage and determination to achieve our dreams. You can do that, too."

"Don't be afraid. We'll always be here for you, Penny," said Harriet Tubman.

"Is Wren here?" I asked.

"Yes, we saw his picture in the other room," came Parker's voice from behind me.

I spun around to see him rubbing his eyes. Then I turned back to look at the rest of my family, but they were gone.

Parker was still yawning and stretching. Since he didn't say anything about all the people in the basement, I decided not to mention it. Knowing what I had to do, I sighed. "Parker, you're right. We've got to leave this place." *I'm sorry, Mama. I didn't do a good job looking after Parker, like you asked me to.*

"We're leaving?" He raised his arms in the air. "Yahoo!"

"I don't know what's going to happen. I don't know if we'll be split up. But I was wrong thinking this was the best solution."

Parker scooted over on his butt and wrapped his arms around me. "Thanks, Penny." He froze for a moment, then hopped up and went over to the side of the basement that was filled with old equipment and boxes.

"What are you doing? Let's get packed."

"Wait," he hollered. "Something that's missing is over here."

What could possibly be down here in the basement that someone was missing?

He came back holding a dusty shoebox. "I think this is Wren's."

I jumped to my feet. "Are you kidding me?"

"Nope." Parker sat next to me and handed me a small photograph from the top of the box. It was a school photograph of a boy with shiny, black hair and a million freckles, just like mine. He looked younger than he had in the painting.

Parker held out his hand, so I gave the picture back. "He looks a lot like you, Penny, but we've got the same hair." Parker set down the picture and pulled a manila folder from the box. He flipped it open. "Just a bunch of paperwork." He set it down.

"Let me see that." I opened the folder and saw a form. It was from the orphanage, and I read the information out loud for Parker. "Baby Boy Doe. Seven pounds, four ounces. 20.5 inches long. Mother—unknown. Father—unknown. Found abandoned on the doorstep of North Carolina General Hospital."

"His parents just left him there?" Parker asked.

"That's what abandoned means," I told him. The box also had a few report cards—he got mostly Cs and Bs. There were some pencils and a drawing pad with a few pages of drawings. Mostly animals. There wasn't much else in the box, but we'd take it with us. Seemed wrong to leave Wren's belongings down here in a dusty basement. That would be like abandoning him again.

I wanted to say goodbye to him before we left. "Start getting our stuff together. I'll be right back," I told Parker. I went back to the room with all the paintings and stared at his face once more, looking for anything I might have missed. His picture didn't give me any idea who his people might be. Could be black or Hispanic or American Indian. He was a mix, like me. A mystery. Magnificent,

like Mama once said. Still, it felt like a thousand questions suddenly stopped spinning, the answers settling in
the hollows of my bones.

But now other questions were popping up. Like
where would me and Parker go now?

CHAPTER 26

We gathered our things, adding Wren's box to our wagon. My watch said it was just after nine a.m. It was Sunday, so the town hall would be closed. "We'll head to the diner and see who's there to help us, then come back for our stuff."

Parker took my hand and we climbed the stairs together up out of the basement of New Hope's Finest.

No one was inside the Finest as we walked outside, but a few strangers were milling around the yard, looking at the tire sculptures and sitting in the chairs. We walked down the driveway to Main Street and saw a big group of folks circled together in front of the diner. I thought for a moment they were all tourists, but on second look, it was all people from town: Joe, Carly's mom, Chase's parents, the Carlsons, and others, too. I widened my eyes, surprised. Some two dozen people gathered in front of the diner on a Sunday morning wasn't a normal thing.

Then Joe turned and looked our way. "There they are!"

Everyone else looked our way, too.

I looked behind me and Parker, wondering who was following us, but no one was there.

As I did so, everyone rushed over to us, Mr. and Mrs. Carlson at the front of the pack. "Where have you two been?" Mrs. Carlson cried as she ran up to us and set one hand on my shoulder and one on Parker's, like she was checking to make sure we were really there.

"You kids all right?" Mr. Carlson asked.

"We were worried sick!" the mayor said, placing her hand on her chest.

I couldn't make any words come out of my mouth, so I just nodded yes.

"We thought something horrible had happened to you!" Joe said.

"We've been living in the basement of the Finest so we wouldn't get split up," Parker said. He turned to the Carlsons. "We're awful hungry. Any pie at your place?"

I nudged him with my elbow. "Mind your manners." I turned back to the crowd. "We're sorry. We wanted to leave before we got shipped off to separate foster homes. We were meaning to live in the mountains, but Parker pointed out that we belonged in the orphanage, and I decided the basement was a better bet than the wild."

"It wasn't," Parker said. "We're out of food, and it's boring down there."

"We've had search parties out looking for you children," Mr. Smith said, sounding angry. "We were just getting set to head out again."

"I'm sorry. We didn't mean to worry anyone," I said. "We didn't think anyone would miss us."

"You seriously think no one in this town would care that Penny and Parker Porter just up and disappeared?" Carly's mom said.

"After losing all those kids from the orphanage, we couldn't lose you, too," Mr. Gaiser said.

Mrs. Carlson raised an eyebrow and looked at Mr. Carlson. He nodded. She knelt beside me and rubbed my back. "Everything is going to be all right. You and Parker can stay with us for a while until we figure this out."

I nodded. *For a while. Not forever.* "We have to get our stuff from the basement. And from Grauntie's."

"She's been worried, too," Mrs. Carlson said.

"I'll take you to Grauntie's, then over to the Carlsons," Joe said.

"Excellent," Mrs. Carlson said. "We'll go get ready for you."

おttt

"I don't know why I didn't think to look in the basement," Joe said as we drove toward Grauntie's.

"Turns out it wasn't such a good idea," I said.

"I almost starved to death," Parker said.

Joe chuckled.

The grass looked so green along the roadside. I suppose locking yourself away for a few days makes the world look different. So does learning what I did while we were down there. I looked at my arms; the color was coming back. "We found a room filled with paintings on the walls. What is that room?"

Joe smiled. "The color-outside-the-box room."

"Why did kids paint down there?" I asked, my throat tight. "They didn't get locked in it, did they?"

"No, never. That was a place to go to when we were feeling sad, or feeling too rambunctious for the world. A place where we could sing at the top of our lungs, or dance past midnight, or paint without wondering who would see it. A place to let our dreams loose. To let our creativity flow."

I nodded. "I saw a painting of our mother down there. One of those paintings you told me Wren could paint that looks like a picture."

He smiled. "He loved her. I know that. Said his life had changed forever when he met her."

"So they had a happy time together, for a while," I said. That was something to be glad about.

卌

"Hello, children," Grauntie said when we walked in. "I have a chore sheet around here somewhere."

Lonnie rushed over and hugged us. "We didn't know what to do when we found you were missing! Your Grauntie was so worried, weren't you?"

Grauntie blinked a few times. "But they're right here."

"We're fine. And we're sorry." I hung my head. "But we're not going to be in your hair anymore. They're finding us a new home. So, thanks for taking care of us. We're going to get our things."

"Can you look for my pocketbook?" she asked.

It was on the kitchen table, so I handed it to her. "You should just keep this right on your lap all the time so you don't lose it."

She tapped her head. "Good idea, Darlene."

There was no denying it: Grauntie was getting worse. It's sad to see someone's memory unspool like that. I heaved a sigh and admitted to myself that it was a good thing she'd be going to a home where someone could take care of her. Where she'd be safe. Parker and I certainly couldn't take care of her and the house *and* ourselves. I leaned over and gave her a kiss—something I'd never done before. Then I gathered my last things and walked away.

Parker was all smiles when we got to the Carlsons. "Can we play music before dinner again? Can we have Thanksgiving in summer again? And pie? Please, please, please can we have pie?"

I glared at him, but he just ignored me.

"Don't you worry. We'll have a good time," Mr. Carlson said.

"We're just staying for a while," I whispered to him. *Don't get too excited*, I reminded myself.

Parker curled up on the couch with a bowl of grapes and permission to watch whatever he wanted on the television.

I grabbed my book from Mr. Hanes to read, but my eyes couldn't settle on the words to make sense of anything. I didn't yet know all these stories by heart, seeing as how the book was so new I'd only read it through once. Still, it felt nice to have a solid thing in my hands, like I was doing something besides fretting. Even if Mrs. Carlson was being honest about keeping us here until we found a home that would take us both, it still meant we were going away. A new town, where we might start having the same old problems as the other places. New Hope just felt like home, especially now that I knew Mama had met Daddy here. That Daddy was still here, if we wanted to visit his grave.

I looked around the Carlsons' living room, out the big, open window that showed off the flowers in their garden. Soft blankets covered the chairs. Beautiful paintings hung on the walls. It was so bright and airy. Seemed like bits of conversation and laughter hung in the air. I got up off the couch and sat in a hard, wooden chair so I wouldn't get too cozy. I could not let myself get used to staying at the Carlsons'.

All day long, folks stopped by to make sure we were all right. Some brought food. Everyone hugged us. Never knew so many people cared. I was exhausted by the time I crawled into bed.

I flicked on the light and pulled out my family tree. I could picture exactly where I'd put the Carlsons if I could: right at the top of it. "I wish they wanted us," I whispered.

"Maybe you should tell them that."

My head snapped up and I saw a woman standing at the end of my bed, with long black hair and an animal skin dress. "Sacagawea?" I whispered. I couldn't believe this was happening again.

She smiled and nodded. "You're brave like me, Penny. Tell the Carlsons what you want."

"I'm not dreaming, am I?" I said.

"No."

"And I wasn't dreaming in the basement?"

"We were all there, too," she said.

My mouth hung open, and I gripped the edge of my comforter—

"If there's something you want, you just have to keep trying until you get it right. That's what I did," said a man's voice beside me. "I tried about a thousand different times until I got the light bulb right. A thousand."

I turned, and there was Thomas Edison.

I pressed my hands against my eyes then opened them, but there were even more people in my room: Frida Kahlo, Martin Luther King, Jr., Rosa Parks. Booker T. Washington was back, too.

"Why does this keep happening? Am I going crazy?" I whispered. The Carlsons wouldn't want a crazy girl who talked to dead people and saw folks in shades of colors. *And they wouldn't want a girl whose father killed their daughter.* "You guys aren't real."

"Excuse me, I'm very real," Thomas Edison said. "I'm in hundreds of textbooks. Probably thousands."

"But you're dead."

"We're very much alive in your imagination," Sacagawea said.

"So I'm imagining you're here right now?"

Frida Kahlo, the painter, walked over. "There's a lot of creative energy in this place. In this town, especially recently. A person's creations hold power. The things they do, too, become a force that lasts over time. And you, Penny. Your imagination comes to life in ways other people's don't. Look at what you created down the road at that old building. That's there today because of you and your creativity. There's nothing wrong with you, Penny."

I nodded slowly. "Most folks don't like when people

are different like that. The Carlsons probably wouldn't. Plus, they already said they didn't want us."

"But you haven't told them that *you* want *them*," Sacagawea said. "You have to ask."

I shook my head so hard it hurt. "No. I won't. Mama told me not to ask for help."

"I think your mama meant well, but, believe me, you need to ask for help," Ida said. "I needed help from family and friends raising my brothers and sisters."

"But a family should just want you, no asking required," I said.

"Sometimes people don't know what they want, what they need," Frida said. "And maybe they don't know how important it is to you. How much you'd like to be with them. How can they make a proper decision without knowing that?"

I couldn't believe what she was suggesting. Tell the Carlsons we wanted to stay here. Ask to be part of a family? That's not how it worked. "What if they say no?" I asked.

"Then you'll know. And you can move on and find a new solution. You won't be stuck forever wondering *what if* . . ." said Ida B. Wells.

I thought about that for a moment. "I guess asking for a place to stay isn't that hard." I curled up on my side in bed. "I'll think about it. Am I going to see you guys again?"

"If you need to. We're always here," Martin Luther King, Jr. said.

A peaceful feeling washed over me, and I lay down again. "I wish you all really were on my family tree."

"Excuse me?" Daniel Boone said. "I am right there next to Gandhi. Didn't my trading inspire you? I know all about your cart."

"Of course it did," I said.

"I saw the many different ways you used those plastic bottles. I know I played a part there," George Washington Carver said.

Clara Barton said, "There are many different kinds of families, Penny. We're happy to be part of yours."

"And I'd say you've built another wonderful family right here with all the townsfolk in New Hope," Ida added. "Those people care about you. Look at everyone who showed up today. And you changed their lives for the better with that project. You belong here."

I wanted to talk more, but my eyelids were so, so heavy.

"So, you're going to ask the Carlsons if they'll have you as their own?" Sacagawea asked.

I nodded, my eyes still closed. "I have to."

CHAPTER 27

Parker was up before me, sitting at the kitchen table with a fork in his hand. "French toast and sausages for breakfast, Penny!"

"Yum," I said, but my stomach was uneasy. It may seem like an easy thing to ask someone if they want you. It's just a few words to spit out, after all. A sentence, maybe two. But I was more scared than I'd ever been. Wobbly-legged-I-might-throw-up scared.

I slid into a chair next to Parker.

"You okay, sweetie?" Mrs. Carlson asked.

I nodded, wondering when would be the right time to have our discussion. The words just weren't coming to me.

I shut my eyes, and I could see my family tree and all the wonderful people standing around it. Rosa Parks smiled in my mind. "Things don't change on their own, Penny. You need to let your voice be heard. Sometimes you do that with your actions, and sometimes you do that with your words. Use your words, Penny."

"You can do it," said Dr. King.

Nodding, I opened my eyes. I had to take a chance. I cleared my throat and gripped my chair. "Mrs. Carlson?"

"Yes, dear?"

The words were frozen on my tongue. "I . . . I have to use the bathroom."

"Go right ahead."

Bolting from my chair, I ran to the bathroom and slammed the door behind me. I leaned up against the door and slid down to the floor, wrapping my arms around my knees. This was ridiculous. I had a family tree full of people to draw inspiration from. All those people who had done incredible things, and I couldn't say a few measly words? Ask for what I wanted more than anything? Some of those people on my tree suffered and fought and worked so hard for what they wanted, and all I had to do was walk down the hall, look Mrs. Carlson in the eye, and share the truth singing in my heart: I wanted us to be a family.

I rested my chin on my knees and noticed my bare feet. Seemed wrong to be asking such an important question in bare feet, so I went to my room and put on socks. But wearing just socks didn't seem right either, so I slipped on some shoes, which seemed very strange with my nightgown. So I took that off and put on a fresh pair of pants and my favorite shirt. I couldn't look like a ragamuffin while asking to be part of someone's family.

I wrung my hands. This was going against everything Mama had told me.

Hands shaking, I pulled her letter out of my nightstand and read it over again. My heart slowed a bit, reading over her words. They calmed me. But I paused as I got to the end:

> I left my mama in charge of you two for now. My family promised to always take care of you both when I'm gone, so you won't have to go into the system.

I folded her letter up again. Mama said her family would take care of us to keep us from going into the system. But they broke that promise; they weren't taking care of us. She probably never imagined that would happen. So what was I supposed to do?

I'm breaking one of your rules Mama, but I have to. If I'm going to look out for Parker and keep us together forever, I have to.

Slowly, I opened the bedroom door. I stood in the hall for a minute. Then I walked toward the kitchen with feet made of cement, until I was standing in front of Mrs. Carlson. I stood there so long, she finally asked me, "Is everything all right?"

Parker blinked at me and stopped chewing.

It was now or never. I took a deep breath, and without thinking too much about the right words to use, I said, "Mrs. Carlson, I think you and Mr. Carlson and me and Parker would make a great family. A forever family. Can we all be a family?"

Parker dropped his fork. Mrs. Carlson stood holding her spatula in the air.

Then she turned around, slid a piece of French toast out of the pan, and turned off the stove. "What do you mean, Penny?"

I swallowed hard. "I think we'd all be happy living together. As a family. We want you to be our mom and dad."

She folded her hands in front of her and looked at the floor. "Penny, we tried bringing in a child once before, and it just didn't work."

What a wallop to my belly. I closed my eyes, hoping tears wouldn't slip out. My heart was out of the box, torn wide open, beating and thumping with hope, and Mrs. Carlson didn't want it.

I could see my family again behind my closed eyes. "No, no, no. Don't give up!" Ida B. Wells said, shaking her finger at me. "Tell her what we all know. You're wonderful. Any family would be lucky to have you."

"Tell her," Sacagawea said, with a knowing smile that calmed my nerves some.

I opened my eyes, squared my shoulders, and looked right into Mrs. Carlson's soft, brown eyes. "Mr. Carlson told us about that. That you think you couldn't take in any kids again. But Parker and I are different. We won't cause any trouble. We've been doing everything at Grauntie's, and we can help here, too. I'll make you tons of tin can critters for free. Honest. We'll help at the diner, too. Whatever you need, we'll do it."

Tears rolled down Mrs. Carlson's face. "I know you kids would be good. But adding new children to the family feels like we're trying to replace Mary, and that's just not right. It's not fair to her. I fear it would leave me with such sadness. And that wouldn't be good for you two, either."

My shoulders slumped. I didn't know how to answer that. I closed my eyes again.

I could see Daniel Boone in my mind now. "Don't

give up now, Penny," he said. "You know why the Carlsons would be happy with you. Tell her."

While Mrs. Carlson did leave the diner that one time we came in, her mood almost always brightened when we were around her. We didn't always make her sad. I tipped up my chin. I had to explain this to her, even if she thought I was crazy. "When me and Parker come to see you and Mr. Carlson, the two of you blaze full color."

She blinked at me a few times. "I'm sorry, dear, I don't understand."

I sighed. "Now, this is going to sound weird, but I see people in shades. When they're happy, when their energy is strong, they're in full color. It changes all the time. Lots of folks around here mope around in black and white. You and Mr. Carlson are always right in the middle—until Parker and I show up. You turn full color when we're around. So you might think we make you sad, but we don't. We make you happy. I see it. And I imagine you probably feel it."

Mrs. Carlson looked at me with misty eyes and nodded. "I do."

"It happened at the Finest, too. You swore you'd never step foot there, but when you did, your color bloomed. You came to love working at the Finest. It's not such a sorrowful place for you anymore. And I think it would be the same if you kept me and Parker. The sad past would get dimmer and dimmer, because we have a big bright future to look forward to—together."

Mrs. Carlson was weeping, but it didn't seem like a sad cry. I wasn't quite sure what to do.

Mr. Carlson came in the front door with a newspaper tucked under his arm. He looked around at us, and his smile faded. He set down the paper. "Now, what is going on in here?"

Mrs. Carlson swiped the back of her hand across her face to catch her tears. "Oh, I just don't know."

I cleared my throat and braced for him to holler at me. "I told Mrs. Carlson that the four of us would make a fine family. We don't want to leave New Hope. Parker and I want to stay with you."

Mr. Carlson's eyes got wide and he puffed out his cheeks. "I thought I explained things to you kids."

"I know. But I don't think you know how much we'd really love to be with you. Forever. I know it's bad manners to ask. And for a long time I thought I shouldn't ask for anything. But someone in my family recently told me you have to ask for what you want. The world doesn't change unless you do something about it. I guess I'm realizing now that it's in my blood—asking for what I want. For what I need: a family. A real one."

Mr. Carlson glanced at his wife. His eyes looked small and sad. "Penny . . ."

Mrs. Carlson's shoulders were bobbing as she sniffled and sobbed. She ran toward me and pulled me into her arms. "Oh, you're right. Of course you're right. We would make a perfect family." She squeezed me tight. "I've thought about it many times, but I've been scared."

My mouth dropped open but I didn't know what to say. Parker, either. His eyes were wide as he sat frozen, watching us.

Mrs. Carlson stepped back and beamed at me. She was blazing in the deepest colors I'd ever seen. "Mr. Carlson and I spend so much time talking about the two of you anyway, it wouldn't be that different to have you here with us. Isn't that right?"

Mr. Carlson looked Mrs. Carlson in the eyes and slowly nodded. "I've always wanted to hear the laughter of kids in our house again. I can't think of two finer children to call our own."

Mrs. Carlson smiled. Really smiled, so that she glowed like I'd never seen. The corners of her mouth reached up to the sky.

Mr. Carlson looked at her and set his hand over his heart. He gathered her into his arms. "There's that smile I've been missing."

Parker popped up from his seat and ran over to hug Mr. Carlson. Mrs. Carlson wrapped an arm around me, and I fell into that hug. I let it swallow me whole and coil up inside me. It was the best hug of my life.

After breakfast, Mrs. Carlson got on the phone with the social services lady to get things in order so we could stay here—for good.

I never knew my heart could feel quite as big as it did at that moment. Probably the way a balloon feels right before it bursts.

I spent the day unpacking my clothes and putting them away in the pretty white dresser in my room.

"This was Mary's room." I looked up, and Mrs. Carlson was standing in the doorway.

"It's nice. Real nice. Does it bother you that I'm in here?"

She tilted her head and paused. "No. It's wonderful to see it being used again. I'm glad it'll be home to such a deserving girl. I'll make us some lunch. Be ready in a bit." She smiled and left me sitting there repeating her words in my head.

"Such a deserving girl," she'd said. But was I? Mrs. Carlson didn't know everything about me. She didn't know everything about my family.

My daddy had killed her daughter.

CHAPTER 29

I went to bed happy, but I still couldn't sleep. Niggling thoughts kept chipping away at the good feelings. Mrs. Carlson's words played over in my head, again and again. *Such a deserving girl.* I must've shifted positions dozens of times. What if things didn't work out with the Carlsons? What if we were too much for them, too? What if she found out about Wren and decided she couldn't keep us? I'd rather never stay here at all if it was going to lead to that. If I got all cozy and settled living here and then was sent away, my heart would crumble into a million pieces.

I flicked on the light and pulled out my family tree. Oh, how I wanted to add the Carlsons to it, right on top. Before I could do that, though, I had to tell Mrs. Carlson everything. And I was pretty sure what she was going to say: "We can't keep you."

My heart was in my throat just thinking about it.

So I grabbed the garbage bag from my trash can and repacked my things. It would be easiest to just scoot right out of the house once she broke the bad news.

I was startled by a rap on my door.

It was Mrs. Carlson. "Penny, can I come in?"

"Okay." I slid the garbage bag onto the floor.

She stepped in the room. "What's got you up so late?"

I noticed my family tree on the bed. "Just thinking."

"There is a lot to think about, isn't there? We're building a new family here. I suppose we'll all have a bit of the jitters as we get to know each other." She noticed my bag on the floor. Her face fell. "Are those your things? Have you changed your mind?"

I swallowed hard and shook my head. "No, but I think you might when you hear what I have to tell you."

"I doubt that, but go ahead. It will feel better to get it out." She sat on the bed next to me.

"There's quite a few things, actually. What if you don't like us when you get to know us better?"

She chuckled softly. "Penny, I know the two of you very well by now. I meant once we get to know each other's habits and quirks."

"We have some odd quirks. I'm afraid we might become too much for you. We usually do."

"Go on."

"For starters, Parker has issues. He can smell things other people can't. Sometimes they set him off into a fit. He can't stand bright lights. He needs to be hugged— a lot."

"That doesn't sound so bad," she said. "I can see what we can do to help him."

"I've got lots of problems, too. And not just seeing people in shades. I've got crooked teeth, and a short temper when people are mean to Parker. And I'm covered in these awful freckles."

"Those aren't awful at all," Mrs. Carlson exclaimed. "They're wonderful. Don't you know what those are?"

"Besides a nuisance?" I shook my head.

"When God sent you down here to this earth, he must've been so pleased with you that he sprinkled you with confetti. Lots of it." She touched the tip of my nose. "Freckles are just God's confetti. And I happen to like them. Especially yours."

I couldn't help but smile. "I like that idea." God's confetti. "But here's a really bad thing. You should know I didn't work so hard to reopen New Hope's Finest as a kindness for the community."

"Oh? Why'd you do it, then?"

"For me and Parker. It's hard to explain, but I just knew if I could get New Hope back on the map, Parker and I could stay here. I was doing it for us, but letting everyone think it was for the town. And in the end, we didn't even get put back on the map."

She was quiet for a moment, staring at me. She looked so sad.

I gulped, waiting for the bad news. She didn't want us. I wasn't deserving after all.

She reached for my hand. "Whatever the reason, you did it. And that's amazing. Doesn't matter why. It may have been a way for you to stay here, but in the end it was a kindness for the community. Everyone found their own personal motivation for working at the Finest. For bringing hope and joy back into their life, trying to put the past behind us."

I smiled. I already felt a whole lot lighter, but then that worried feeling returned. I wasn't done telling her everything. "There's more, though. The other day . . ." I gulped. I closed my eyes and blurted out my secret as quickly as I could. "The people on my family tree came to life and were talking to me, even in this very room. People who are dead." Maybe this would be too much for her, and then I wouldn't even have to tell her the awful truth about Wren. I hung my head. "I'm pretty sure I'm different enough that I would've ended up in the orphanage if it were still open."

Mrs. Carlson held out her hand. "Let me see your family tree."

I handed it to her. "When I was in the basement, they showed up and told me I couldn't stay there." I bit my lip and looked down at the floor. "They were in this room last night, talking to me. I might be crazy."

She smiled as she looked my tree over. "I am certain you are not crazy, Penny. And maybe you did see these people. Maybe they're so alive in your mind that they're with you all the time. I think that's wonderful."

"I don't even know who I am, Mrs. Carlson. I don't know much about my daddy, besides his name. I might be black, I could be Mexican, or Cuban. Maybe American Indian. Doesn't that bother you? That I don't know?"

"Why would it? Besides, I know who you are, Penny."

"You do? How?"

"I know you by the things you do. You're a leader. You're creative. And you're so, so brave, telling me all these things. And it just makes me more sure than ever that bringing you and Parker into our family is exactly what we want to do."

She was making this so hard to tell her the worst truth: the truth about Wren. I called up every bit of bravery I had to get the next words out. There was no way she'd want us after hearing this, but it wasn't fair to keep it a secret. And it would eat away at me every day if she didn't know. I could barely make my voice rise above a whisper. "And there's one very, very bad thing you need to know. And I understand that, when you find out, you probably won't want to keep us. But it's only fair to tell you."

She squared her shoulders. "Okay. I'm ready for whatever it is."

"I just recently figured out who my daddy was: Wren. A boy from the orphanage my mama met that summer. But that wasn't his real name. His real name was . . ." I sucked in a deep breath. "Michael Hope. The man who killed your daughter." Tears streamed down my cheeks, but I looked up into her eyes. I had to see the truth about how she felt.

Her eyes weren't hard and angry. And they weren't surprised, either. They were soft and sad. "I recently figured out that Michael was your father," she said. "Your freckles. When you mentioned your mama stayed here that summer. Long ago, Joe tried to explain to me why

Michael drove off that day. That he was upset about a girl. But I never knew who that girl was."

My eyebrows shot up. "And you don't hate me because of it?"

"Of course not. And I didn't hate him, either."

"Really? Why not?"

"Because it was an accident. He was going too fast, and Mary wasn't paying attention. She was waving to a friend across the street. She actually rode right into his path."

"So he wasn't a totally horrible person?" I asked.

She rubbed my back. "Of course not. One mistake doesn't define a person. It's all the things they do. And there will always be some good and some bad. Unfortunately, he couldn't see that, and he left. And he paid the ultimate price."

I nodded. "He died."

"That's true. But I meant that he paid the ultimate price because he never got to meet you two."

My heart felt like someone was squeezing it. There was hurt and hope and truth all swirled inside it. She was right. We missed out on having a daddy, but he missed out on having us.

She held open her arms. "Come here. I promise you,

there is nothing you or Parker could ever do or say that would make me stop loving you."

My throat was so tight I couldn't say a word. I was worried my heart might burst. I blinked at her through my tears and crawled into her hug, wrapping my arms around her neck and resting my head on her shoulder while she rocked back and forth. "Can I put you on my family tree?" I asked.

She kissed the top of my head. "Of course you can. I'd be honored to be nestled in among all those fine folks who helped you become the lovely girl you are."

I sighed, like every last bit of sadness had finally left me. "You and Mr. Carlson are going right on the top." I was still hugging her. This time, I was going to wait for her to let go.

CHAPTER 30

Mrs. Carlson must have been the one to eventually let go, but I didn't know it until the next morning when I woke up and found myself all tucked in. I finished unpacking my things, for good this time, and noticed the tube with the map in it leaning up against the wall. I sighed. I had been so sure that fixing up the Finest would get us back on the map. I'd felt it in my bones. How had I been so wrong?

I slid the map from the container and smoothed it out on my bed. It'd be so nice to see New Hope listed there.

I paused for a moment. *It can still be listed there*, I thought. *It should be.* I grabbed my pen and picked a spot between Asheville and Winston-Salem. I colored in a big dot and wrote New Hope right next to it. They were the two prettiest words I'd ever seen. My heart filled, seeing our town finally listed there, even if it was only me who put it there. *I am the girl who put her town back on the map.*

I went into the living room, where Mrs. Carlson was reading the newspaper. "Good morning." She flashed me her reach-to-the-heavens smile.

"It is a good morning. And I have a big favor to ask." Couldn't believe I was asking for something else! "Can I hang my map up in my room?"

"Of course. Mr. Carlson can help you with that. We can get a nice frame for it. We'll have to repaint in there, too, and get you a new quilt and decorations. You can pick out whatever you'd like."

My throat was too thick to say anything. That was way more than I could have ever hoped for. "I'm going to go pick out the perfect spot."

I ran back to my room and turned around and around, taking it all in—the two big windows that let in just the right amount of light. The pretty little table next to the bed. *This is my room. This is my home.*

I was sitting on the bed, smiling, when I noticed a scrap of paper on the floor next to it. Cautiously, I picked it up and unfolded it. It was from Charter Maps. I guess it must've been inside the tube with the map. My heart started pounding.

Dear Penny,
    It sounds like you're doing amazing things

in New Hope! We've actually gotten a few calls from people wondering why your town isn't on the map. If we keep getting more calls like that, I'm sure New Hope will be included in our next edition. Keep up the good work!

Sincerely,
Sheila Blakeley
Secretary to CEO David Charter

I looked up at the ceiling and closed my eyes. I pictured that bright slice in the sky from a few weeks ago. Guess my wish really had wiggled its way through to the place where amazing things happen. "I did it. I really did it."

I hurried out to the living room and took the note to show Mrs. Carlson.

She read it and hugged me. "That's wonderful, Penny!" She stepped back and stared at me, lowering her voice to an awed hush. "I can't wait to see all the other amazing things you do."

I beamed, just imagining the wonderful life waiting for me.

Parker wandered out of his bedroom, rubbing his eyes.

"Guess what?" I said. "We're probably getting back on the map next time they print a new one."

"You did it!" he cried. "Just like you said you would."

"We did it. We all did it," I said.

I looked down, and my hands were glowing. My color was brighter than ever before.

ⅢⅢ

After breakfast, the four of us walked down to the Finest, just to look around. It felt nice being there, especially being there together.

A tour bus was parked along Main Street, and people were wandering up to New Hope's Finest.

"I can't believe people are still stopping for a look," I said.

"I want to take another walk around. Seems like I notice something different each time I'm here," my new mom said.

Mom. Mom. Mom. The word pulsed in my heart.

When we got to the gate, Miss Meriwether was there, telling a group of old folks about the best dishes to order at the diner.

"This is a remarkable place," said a man walking out the gate.

"None of it would've happened without our Penny," Mom said, settling her hands on my shoulders. "It was her idea to turn this old eyesore into something new and bring life back to the town. There was no hope here for a long while. But she brought it back." She beamed down at me. "She is our hope."

Those were just about the kindest words I'd ever heard.

The man looked at me and put his hands on his hips. "You're Penny?"

I nodded.

"You did all this?"

"I had some help." From everyone in town. From the great people on my family tree.

"But Penny started everything. Without her, this never would've happened," Mom said.

The man smiled at me. "Guess you're a lucky penny."

"I'm not lucky," I said, without thinking. But then I clamped my mouth shut. Maybe that was changing now.

"I meant you're the town's lucky penny," he said. "They're lucky to have you."

I blinked a few times, 'cause tears were pricking the

back of my eyes. "Come on, let's go look at it all." I raced for the tree house, with Parker and Mr. and Mrs. Carlson following me. My mom and dad.

Forgetting my crooked teeth, I smiled wide, like I'd never smiled before. I turned around and saw all the folks from my family tree standing behind me in the yard, waving at me.

"We'll be here whenever you need us," Sacagawea said.

Miss Ida nodded. "But it looks like you're in good hands for now."

I waved to them, then turned to look up at the tree house before climbing the stairs. For just a second, I thought I saw a flash of copper-colored hair and a splotch of freckles.

My whole family was finally here together in New Hope.

ACKNOWLEDGMENTS

I am so very grateful to the many people who helped bring this book to life. To my agent, Jennifer Unter, thanks for finding it a wonderful home. To my editor, Rachel Stark, your amazing feedback helped turn this story into something even more special. Thank you so much to Abby Stroman, and Ella and Sara Manurung for your perspective on growing up mixed-race. Jennifer Galyon answered a lot of questions about growing up in a small town in North Carolina in the early 1980s. Thank you! Anne Siconolfi from Hillside Children's Center gave me helpful information on the foster care system.

And sadly, as I wrote this book, I experienced a first-hand account of dementia, as my mother's memory slips away, very much like Grauntie's. It's been devastating to watch her go from forgetting her purse to forgetting who I am. I'm heartsick that my mother will never be able to read this book, will never be able to tell me she loves me again. If only I had a letter from my mom like Penny does, telling me how to go on without her. Thank you for being a great mother, and for making me believe I could do anything.